THE PERFECT SUBMISSIVE

THE PERFECT SUBMISSIVE

Kay Jaybee

Published by Xcite Books Ltd – 2012

ISBN 9781908262783

Printed and bound in the UK by CPI Group (UK) Ltd, Croydon, CR0 4YY

Cover design by
Sarah Ann Davies

My love and thanks to S and my family, for their never-ending support.

I am also grateful to AE, AMH, BH and DB for their constant encouragement and friendship, despite their occasional bewilderment at my choice of career.

Special mention must go to my writing right arm, K D Grace – without whom I would have gone insane and got a 'proper' job long ago!

Finally, I must thank my sources of inspiration – you know who you are.

Chapter One

LAURA PETERS' MIND WENT into overdrive. Flicking through a variety of possible erotic scenarios, she placed him at the mercy of a large muscular man, begging to be skewered up the arse on his magnificent cock. She saw him bound and gagged; a darkly tanned figure bent over his chest, stroking him relentlessly with a split-tailed whip. Perhaps he was writhing on a four-poster bed, awaiting a woman's eager tongue against his balls; a woman who'd just spent the last hour teasing his body with silk scarves …

Snapping her mind back to reality, the manageress glanced at the wooden-cased grandfather clock that stood behind the hotel bar. It was a couple of minutes to 11 p.m. and the poised man at the corner table, who'd sparked her imagination so powerfully, had been watching her for a least half an hour.

Sitting alone on a padded stool, her back resting against the bar, Laura could clearly picture the thoughts running through his mind. *Is she an escort or a prostitute? A business woman travelling alone to a conference? Does she have a partner about to join her?* She knew it wouldn't occur to him that she was the co-runner of the Fables Country Hotel in which he was staying.

Shaking out the long russet hair that hung down her

neck, Laura felt it smother her shoulders. Fixing her bright green eyes on one of the ghastly paintings that adorned the hotel lounge's walls, she hid her smile as the guest continued to observe her. She wondered when he would make a move. He was, or appeared to be, exactly what she was looking for.

Without giving the stranger the satisfaction of seeing her glance at him in return, Laura mentally weighed up his appearance. At approximately 5' 9", he was only an inch taller than her, and she guessed his age to be in the region of 35. His short-sleeved shirt revealed his arms to be muscular without being overworked, and as he sipped at his pint of beer she noticed the signs of a small tattoo peek from beneath his casually smart polo-shirt sleeve, although she was unable to see precisely what it depicted. Reining in her thoughts from too much speculation as to the nature and extent of his body art, Laura continued her silent summary of his physical attributes.

The short brown hair that framed a roughly shaved face was speckled with the first flecks of grey. Almost square in shape, his rugged confident face held deep brown eyes. Those eyes seemed to hold so much promise, and Laura felt a frisson of lust trip down her spine as she wondered what it was going to feel like when he locked them on to her own and begged her to make him come, pleaded with her to … Laura took a deep breath. She was convinced that it would happen, and was already quietly looking forward to seeing how he would cope with what she had in mind.

Sipping her drink, Laura wondered how he saw her, with her ankle-length khaki-green dress gathered beneath her chest in a style reminiscent of a character from Jane Austen. On a slimmer or shorter female it would have looked wrong, but on her tall Rubenesque figure, the

2

result was simply stunning. Perfectly proportioned, she was beautifully rounded and gorgeously curved.

Continuing to covertly watch the stranger, Laura reflected on how at ease he seemed compared to many of the business men and women who passed through the doors of the hotel. His features didn't display the slightest trace of anxiety, and the manageress was struck by the man's air of self-possession. It occurred to Laura that he might, from the smirk that played around his lips, be lost in a sexual fantasy. She hoped he was.

Suddenly he turned and stared straight at her. Laura pulled herself away from her own lurid fantasies; already knowing what he intended to say as he rose from his chair and took a step in her direction. To let him speak to her now would be to play by his rules, and if her theory was to be tested then she needed to wrong-foot this man.

Just before he reached her, Laura deliberately put down her semi-consumed drink, and left the room without a backward glance. Ducking through the staff entrance behind the bar, she selected a small white business card from her bag and scribbled a note onto its back. Leaving very clear instructions with the barman to pass the card to the guest once he'd finished his drink, Mrs Laura Peters departed and headed to the hotel's fifth floor, confident that the lateness of the hour meant the man who had so piqued her interest, would still be in the hotel the following morning. Until that time, she had work to do.

Dressing early, in a simply cut black trouser suit and cream silk blouse, Laura left the room that served as her living quarters and headed to Reception to find out a few details about the guest who'd occupied her nocturnal thoughts. Nodding a taciturn greeting to the girl behind the desk, Laura began to scan the hotel's computer records. Forty-three of the hotel's fifty regular rooms were occupied.

A cross between a businessman's stopover hotel, a conference base, and a haven of pampering for the ladies of Oxfordshire, the modern "adult-only" environment of the Fables Hotel was the perfect discreet location for Laura's line of work. Flicking through the spreadsheet that displayed the bookings for the five rooms on the fifth floor, for which she was personally responsible, Mrs Peters smiled at the satisfying clutch of bookings that had already been made for the next few weeks.

Moving back to the list of regular customers, her eyes fell on the details of the delegates who'd attended the artists' conference that had broken up the day before. All but one of the members had departed, a Mr Samuel Wheeler. The length of stay would fit. It might not be him, but somehow Laura was sure that it was. She began to type.

As her work dictated a schedule of continual late nights, the manageress of the fifth floor rarely partook of the Fables first meal of the day, but today Laura was determined to see if the creature that had subjugated himself to her so willingly during her early morning dreams had emerged for breakfast.

He was in the dining room reading *The Telegraph*, while munching on some crisp brown toast. Alone. Picking up a cup of strong black coffee, Laura shoved her shoulders back and walked purposefully over to his table.

Introducing herself as the manageress of the hotel's adult leisure department, she asked if he would mind her joining him for a few moments.

A knowing look crossed the guest's features as he folded up his paper. His voice, as he agreed to her

4

company was unexpectedly husky, as if he had a 40-a-day habit, and yet Laura noticed no faint odour of nicotine hanging about him. With an unmistakably playful twinkle at the corner of his dark eyes, he introduced himself as Sam.

Unspoken words hung in the air between them as he pointed to the chair opposite. Laura ignored his open invitation to sit down, pleased that her private assumption as to his identity had been correct. Although, considering the calm expression on his face, she wondered if her business card and message had been passed on as instructed. She quickly dismissed the doubt. Lee wasn't that stupid, he'd been working behind the bar at Fables for long enough to know what would happen if he didn't do as she requested.

Deciding to trust her initial instincts about Mr Samuel Wheeler's potential, Laura took the newspaper from his grasp, and fixed his eyes with hers. 'I left you my card.' It was a statement not a question.

She studied his face closely while he acknowledged recognition of this fact. His forehead remained un-furrowed, but his voice had an unmistakably questioning lilt. 'I thought it might have been from you, but then I thought not. I didn't see you so much as glance at me last night; you were always looking the other way.'

'I was watching you, watching me.'

The briefest quiver of uncertainly flashed across Sam's face before he regained control. To Laura, the speed at which he recovered his composure was a further point in his favour.

Determined to maintain the upper-hand, Laura continued, 'I'm good at seeing things.'

Sam considered the woman before him with openly hungry speculation. There was an almost stately presence about her, an elegance that screamed control and suggested an innate unquenchable sexuality. In other words, Sam thought as he studied her, this woman is dangerous.

The look the artist was giving her sent a welcome shiver of erotic expectation through the manageress's stomach. 'I'm Mrs Peters – Laura – I will see you this evening. As you'll know, if you read my card, you have an appointment.'

Mr Wheeler looked as though he was going to laugh, but then thought better of it. 'I'm afraid I'm about to book out. I have to go home today.'

'That has already been taken care of. Your stay has been extended for an additional night.'

Again, a second's discomfort crossed his face before Sam said, 'You're a married woman.'

'I use the title for work only. It helps some of my married customers to believe I am cheating too. I am not the marrying kind.'

'I see.' Outwardly recomposed, Sam added, 'I can't, I have to work.'

Laura stared into his eyes for a fraction too long to be comfortable. 'Do you? Are you sure?'

He shifted a little in his seat as Laura continued, enjoying the powerful advantage her height gave her as she peered down. 'You were here for the artists' conference, and yet that is over, and you are still here. It occurs to me, Mr Samuel Wheeler, that you are not really in a hurry to go back to work; perhaps it doesn't make you happy?' His mouth dropped open as Laura went on, 'I on the other hand, love my work, and I can promise you that I am everything I seem and more …'

Departing abruptly, Laura swept from the dining room, her head held high, her hips swaying, every bit the queen of all she surveyed; leaving the artist sitting as if stunned, his pulse beating rapidly, the remains of his neglected toast cooling before him.

Restless with the knowledge that she would have to kill several hours before she could test drive Mr Samuel Wheeler, Laura knew she had to do something to alleviate her body's fast building need.

With a faint smile, she decided that, once her morning session with a regular Fables guest was complete, she would reward herself with a visit to the hotel's cramped booking office.

The Fables employed 30 members of staff in total. Some of them knew about the specialised facilities available on the top floor. The others, if they'd ever thought about it, believed it to be a mixture of staff quarters and store rooms. Jess Sanders knew its real function, but she hadn't known for long.

From the moment she'd decided she was finally sick of temping her way around the offices of Oxford, Jess had applied for every administration post she could find advertised. To her delight, it was only a matter of days before she found herself the administration assistant, booking clerk, and general office hand of the Fables County Hotel.

Laura Peters had seen the new employee's potential for elevation to the fifth floor immediately. The 25-year-old, however, obviously had no idea of the talent that lay hidden within her shapely yet petite body.

With short bobbed red hair framing her round freckled face, habitually lowered pale green eyes, and breasts marginally too big for the tight bra in which she'd encased them, Jess had instantly become an itch Laura wanted to scratch. Quite literally.

Given her position within the hotel's general running, Jess couldn't be sheltered from its extra features once her appointment had been made, and it was with deep interest that Laura Peters observed the girl's face as Mr Davies, manager of the main hotel, calmly informed her of the type of bookings she would be responsible for making, concerning rooms 50 to 54.

'Ladies and gentleman of some means will, on a private telephone number kept separate from the ordinary business line, book the top floor rooms for differing periods of time. Sometimes for an hour, sometimes for a night, occasionally for a period of days. Now and again a customer will request a booking for more than one of the rooms at a time. I should stress that this is not a prostitution racket, nor do we provide escorts. This is a discreet adult entertainment and relaxation service, and everyone involved here wants to be involved. The entertainment staff's services are not specifically paid for, only the rooms and meals as for the rest of the hotel. Do you understand what I'm saying, Miss Sanders?'

Jess had nodded as she took in this information, high points of pink embarrassment colouring her cheeks. Examining the new girl's expression as she took in this unexpected information, Laura frowned thoughtfully. *Was the mystery of exactly what lay hidden behind those five doors turning her on?* She was sure it was, whether Miss Sanders wanted it to or not. As she perched on the edge of the black swivel chair, her chest hadn't been able to hide the extra little heave it gave as Mr Davies deferred to Laura, who began to list each of the extra room's specialities.

'The majority of callers here are regulars, and will ask for the room they require simply by number. However, those new to The Fables might ask, for example, if we have a torture chamber, or a study, and so on. It is important for you to know what facilities we're able to offer.'

Waiting a few silent seconds for Jess to respond, taking some mild pleasure from her discomfort, Laura eventually accepted that no response was forthcoming, and continued in the same matter of fact manner, 'Room 50 contains a dungeon and all the equipment you would expect to find within it. Room 51 is a Victorian-style study. Room 52 is a school room and Room 53 is a hospital examination room. Fairly predictable I'm afraid, but our guests like what they like, and who am I to argue? Room 54 is more unusual, and the contents of the room will remain a secret until the guest sets foot inside.'

Fixing her gaze on the clerk as she fidgeted in her chair, Mrs Peters was convinced that Miss Sanders' knickers were becoming damp. She also noticed that the girl's nipples were visibly poking at her white jumper; a condition totally at odds with the shocked look on her face.

That was the moment Laura knew for sure that she wanted Miss Jess Sanders on her staff. It would take a little training, perhaps a great deal of training ... but the mistress of the fifth floor was sure it would be worth the effort ... natural submissives were so hard to find.

Chapter Two

JESS WAS SITTING AT her desk, a half-eaten sandwich in one hand; the fingers of her other hand dancing over the computer keyboard. Laura watched her through the office window for a few moments before confidently stepping into the room, interrupting the clerk without hesitation. 'Mr Davies informs me he has not yet had time to complete your preliminary tour of the hotel.'

Understanding precisely where the manageress intended to take her, Jess spoke carefully, 'I've seen most of it, but not all.'

Without confirming the clerk's suspicions, Laura said, 'I have a few moments, so if you'd like to walk this way I'll complete that area of your training.' She pointed towards the office door. 'You are bound to be asked for directions around the place by our guests and it doesn't look very professional if a member of staff gets lost herself, wouldn't you agree?'

'I would, Mrs Peters.'

Although she'd now worked at the Fables for just over a week, Jess still hadn't looked her boss in the eye once, a fact that sent a buzz of conviction through Mrs Peters; her initial instincts about the girl had been correct.

'Are you happy here so far, Miss Sanders?'

'Yes, Mrs Peters. Thank you.' Jess muttered her response, almost managing to glance directly at her superior, but falling short at her shoulders. Laura's heartbeat increased in response to the girl's natural deference. Jess Sanders was just so perfect for what she had in mind.

As they walked towards the staff lift Laura attempted to improve the flow of conversation. 'And I don't think you have yet been introduced to all the other members of staff?'

'Not yet, no.' Again Jess spoke cautiously, and Laura knew from the expression on her face that she was both fearful and curious about meeting anyone who kept their business arrangements entirely to the Fables upper storey.

'We are one member of staff down at the moment; one of my assistants has left us for pastures new. I'm searching for a replacement. Master Lee Philips, who works in the bar downstairs, helps me out as and when required, but it's not an ideal arrangement. He has many other duties, and besides, the fifth floor guests frequently prefer the female touch.'

Following the clerk into the lift it was obvious that no small talk was going to come from her, so Laura calmly kept up her commentary. 'My associate, Miss Sarah, should be on the premises by 10.00 each morning, unless she has had a complete night session, in which case she is not expected until 2 p.m. As I've said, Master Philips comes and goes, depending on our requirements and his bar and reception work. Miss Sarah has her first session of the day in a few moments, if we are lucky we should just catch the show.'

Visibly shrinking back, Jess noticed how Mrs Peters walked a little taller now they'd reached her domain. Her face was more set, her back straighter, and somehow she appeared even more intimidating than before. Pushing her hands into the deep pockets of her clinging knee-length black skirt, Jess hid the growing sheen of perspiration on her palms, while trying to ignore the fearful beat of her pulse.

Crossing the threshold of the room, into which she was being firmly steered by the elbow, felt like entering another world to Jess, or rather, another time. Manoeuvred towards a plush red velvet chaise longue, her eyes darting here and there, the clerk was pointedly sitting down.

Trying to ignore the light but persistent pressure of Mrs Peters' cool hand against her wrist, Jess took in the reproduction William Morris wallpaper, the heavy dark-wood chest of drawers, the floor to ceiling bookshelves, and the faded brown leather wing-backed armchair. Centre stage, only a few metres from where they sat, was a huge writing desk. Its top was inlaid with a square of leather, a portion of which was covered with blotting paper, an accompanying ink well, pots of ink, and nibbed pens.

Jess was reminded of a museum she'd once visited as a child, where rooms from a variety of different houses had been re-created from a number of historical periods. This room had Victorian study written all over it.

The silence was beginning to get to her as she waited, perched rather than sat, on the unyielding seat. A faint voice of hope at the back of her head kept telling her that all this had to be some sort of practical joke, but one glance at Mrs Peters made Jess reconsider. Her eyes kept drifting towards the study door. Whatever she had been brought here to witness surely couldn't begin until someone came in. Twenty seconds later, each one ticked off by the hammer of Jess's heart beating, the door swung back with a confident push.

'Ah, Miss Sarah,' Laura rose from her seat, a stern

glare at Jess telling her not to move. 'I hope you don't mind, but Fables has a new member of staff, and I thought it would be a good idea to let her observe one of our sessions.'

Miss Sarah, her face powdered to an ultra-pale complexion, her curling hair pinned up in the style of a Victorian lady, her exquisite outfit historically accurate down to the small white buttons that fastened her stylish black boots, curtsied at once to her superior. 'Of course, Mrs Peters.'

The stunningly slim woman glanced briefly at Jess, her grey gaze only lingering long enough to acknowledge the stranger, without taking in what she looked like or who she might be. Miss Sarah's indifference, dismissing the office clerk as an unimportant factor in the room, made Jess feel smaller and more anxious than ever.

The agonising lull continued and Jess's imagination began to run riot as Miss Sarah sat at the desk in preparation for her client's arrival. Images of pock-skinned overweight men, panting loudly as they fucked the employees of the fifth floor against the furniture made Jess's stomach churn, but there was no way out. With a quiet determination that Mrs Peters would have been surprised to know Jess possessed, she thought, *if the other members of staff here have survived this part of the tour, then so can I.*

As Mrs Peters returned to both the chaise longue and her application of gentle restraint against the clerk's arm, Jess's body stiffened. Someone was knocking on the door. Not daring to face her employer, Jess focused on the figure that, after being granted permission to enter, walked meekly into the study.

If he hadn't had his neck bent, his face to the floor with respect for Miss Sarah, who greeted him with a sharp

13

'Good morning', Jess judged he would have been quite tall. And he was young; not the sweaty, aged bank manager Jess had conjured up in her head, but a man in his late 20s or early 30s, with a shaven face, short spiked ginger hair, and well built limbs. He was dressed as a servant, perhaps a stable hand. Jess was automatically reminded of *Lady Chatterley's Lover*. Gulping against her dehydrated throat, unwilling to see the sex that she was sure was about to follow, the clerk dropped her eyes, only to have her chin roughly jerked upwards by Mrs Peters. 'No, child. You will observe. You will learn.'

A patina of panic gripped Jess. Every hair on the back of her neck stood to attention. Until that moment it had been unreal. She hadn't let go of the hope that at any minute someone was going to turn around and say, 'OK, Jess, it's just a joke. We play it on all the new girls. Let's grab a coffee.' No one did though. No one was saying anything.

The suffocating quiet of the room was broken by the newcomer, who apparently totally oblivious to his audience, was pressed to his knees by Miss Sarah. His head lowered, he was left where he was as the lady sat in the wing-backed chair, her back straight, her chin tilted, her clear eyes filled with disdain as she studied her supplicant.

Jess tried to turn her head away for a second time, but again, had it sharply wrenched back to the scene unfolding before her. She felt incredibly hot despite the general chill of the room, and wished she could take off the thick jumper that was so essential in her cold little bookings office.

Miss Sarah stood again, her abrupt movement making Jess jump and Mrs Peters smile with sardonic approval. 'You know why I have called you here, Master Paul.'

14

'Yes, my lady.' The words were spoken with humility, but Jess heard every word. It was like being in a theatre watching someone dictating well rehearsed lines.

'I believe I've had to speak to you before about your time-keeping. Twice before in fact.'

The man's eyes remained dipped. 'Yes, my lady.'

'I'm afraid that, as this is not the first time there has been cause to reprimand you, the punishment will be more severe this time.' Miss Sarah didn't sound afraid at all. Her cut-glass voice sounded triumphant as she towered over the man, who seemed to be getting smaller, as if he was shrinking against her tone.

With a rustle of the petticoats hidden beneath her bust hugging dress, Miss Sarah turned from her client and began to search through the desk drawer. Jess held her breath; positive she knew what Miss Sarah was searching for. *It has to be a wooden ruler.* Jess had read enough erotica to know how these scenarios went. It was almost text book. She wondered if she should have been disappointed, but the hardening of her nipples told her otherwise, as did the tell-tale twitch beneath her skirt. Determined to keep her unbidden arousal secret, Jess privately admonished herself for being so susceptible.

She averted her eyes from the woman at the desk, but Jess couldn't bring herself to turn them from the manservant. He captivated her. So strong, so masculine. *What makes him want to come here and be controlled like this? Why does he pay to be humiliated?*

'It's fascinating, isn't it?' Mrs Peters seemed to be reading her mind.

Jess felt goose pimples sprinkle her flesh as her employer continued to speak in whispers, her warm breath tickling Jess's ear, 'He's a strong young man. He is good-looking. He could dominate any girl he chose, and

15

yet here he is, getting his rocks off by crouching in obedience before a powerful woman.'

Jess opened her mouth to speak, but no words came out. She didn't know what to say; or even if she was permitted to speak. Instead she flicked her attention back to Miss Sarah, who'd finished her deliberately protracted hunt through the desk, and now held, not a ruler, but a short handled white whip.

'Assume the position, Master Paul.' Miss Sarah stood proud, the whip resting naturally in her palm, as the young man approached the desk and dropped his breeches.

He was about to place his chest against the desk, when Miss Sarah interrupted him. 'I think today, as we have visitors, you should move to the other side of the desk.'

Her guest looked up, his face crimson as he allowed himself to properly register the presence of Jess and Mrs Peters for the first time.

Master Paul said nothing as he shuffled awkwardly forward, his clothing around his ankles, giving Jess her first glance of his rigid cock. She released an involuntary sigh as she saw it; tight, textured, its smooth tip glistening with want. Jess didn't think she'd ever seen a man so turned on. To her surprise, she realised she would have felt disappointed if she hadn't been able to see his dick.

'Magnificent isn't he?' Mrs Peters appeared amused as she regarded the clerk, the fingers around her wrist allowing her to feel every beat of Jess's fastening pulse. 'I think you should pay close attention, Miss Sanders. If the speed at which your blood is pumping is anything to go by, you are going to enjoy this.'

Jess's face flushed as red as Paul's had done. She felt as though she had been found out, even though, until that moment, she wouldn't have dreamed that seeing a man so willingly humbled would have such a profound physical effect on her. As liquid began to seep through her silk panties, Jess hung her own head in shame, yet her wide green eyes remained raised, and fixed upon the subject of chastisement.

Hastened into position by his mistress, Paul's shirt was torn from his back, his smooth torso bent over the desk's leather inlay, and his outstretched muscular arms grasped each side of the desktop. Jess gasped at the sight of his arse. It was truly gorgeous. She was so close to him, only two metres away. She could smell his desire and almost taste the frisson of fear that ran down his spine; prone and vulnerable, as he anticipated the first strike.

Balling her hands into fists, Jess's fingernails dug into the flesh of her palms as she waited in unexpected harmony with the man before her. Miss Sarah, standing behind her victim, undid the top three buttons that held her dress taut across her chest. After allowing her lungs to inflate properly for the first time since her bodice was fastened, she swung her right arm high and cracked the whip down against Master Paul's backside.

Yelping as the strike scored a pink welt against his skin the guest held the desk harder, but he didn't move as Miss Sarah threw her arm back for a second time, and then a third, building up a neat criss-cross pattern on his rump.

Suddenly realising that she had been holding her breath while mentally counting the strikes, Jess exhaled in a protracted measured wave, trying to relax her hands, painfully aware that her wrist was still in her superior's iron clutch.

As the fifth and sixth strokes slammed down, the new clerk found she was listening intently to every sound, fascinated as Master Paul's whimpers morphed into muted cries and whimpers. *What would that feel like? Why does he like it?* On the eighth strike Miss Sarah hesitated, her arm poised in the air, the whip hovering menacingly. 'Are you sorry, Master Paul?'

'Yes, my lady, I'm sorry.' He spoke through gritted teeth, his words escaping into a pleading moan as the crop hit again.

'How sorry?' Altering the angle of the weapon, the ninth stroke landed with fearful accuracy upon the very crack of his buttocks. Jess winced, biting back a sympathetic cry of her own, as Master Paul screamed, 'I'm very sorry, my lady. Very very sorry.'

'And will it happen again? Will you be late for your duties from now on?'

Unconscious of her actions, so caught up was she in Master Paul's punishment, Jess leant forward, her mouth dry, her lips parted. *Surely there will be one more strike to take the number to ten?*

'You are correct, child. There will be another hit.'

Jess started, drawing herself back. *How could I have forgotten Mrs Peters, even for a second? And how the hell does she know what I'm thinking?*

Still not brave enough to look at her superior, Jess lowered her gaze again, ashamed of her own curiosity. This time, however, her face wasn't yanked back up, and she was not physically coerced into viewing the erotic tableau being played out before her, and it was with a sense of personal shock that Jess realised she was disappointed by this. She wanted to see what would happen next, but she knew that she needed to be made to watch. This was not how she'd been brought up. This was wrong. She had always been the good girl and Jess wasn't willing to admit to herself that she was enjoying what she saw. Mrs Peters knew though. Jess knew she knew, and the thought made her shiver.

As she stared at the wooden floor Jess could hear the sound of a dress being undone. Then Miss Sarah's frock hit the floor with the weighty thud of expensive material. Not wanting to raise her head and make her interest blatant, Jess slid her eyes up as far as she they would go. Resting her gaze on some far from Victorian underwear, Jess swallowed at the sight of the woman's bright red suspenders and black stockings, which ran up from the buttoned high heeled boots to a scarlet bustle. Her eyes widened as she took in the bare peach backside, which turned to reveal a clean-shaven mound of cream silken skin.

The temptation was too great; Jess had to see more. Trying to ignore Mrs Peters' satisfied mutterings, the clerk lifted her head and was rewarded by the vision of the most perfect pair of breasts she'd ever seen. The only pair of breasts she had ever seen in real life in fact. She shuddered at the effect they had on her body, a body that was contradicting its wants with fear, as she sat, frozen with uncertainty, her brain battling to accept what she had seen, what she was seeing, the unreal position she had been put in, and the birth of a desire she never knew she possessed.

Jess was aware that Miss Sarah was talking to Master Paul again, but the view of the semi-naked couple before her, and the knowledge of the fast warming hand against her clammy skin, drowned out the sound of the woman's words. It was only the servant's abrupt cries turning to begs, that made Jess gather in her confused thoughts and concentrate on what was happening.

'Please, Miss Sarah, please hit me again.' Master Paul's voice crackled with yearning. 'I want my final sting. I *need* it, my lady'. Miss Sarah trailed the very end of the whip over his back then, lowered herself onto her haunches, her face now level with her client's. 'And will you give me what I desire in return?'

'Oh yes, my lady, I will.' The sentence left Master Paul's lips in a mad rush. It was as if they were the words he'd been longing to say from the moment he'd first entered Room 51.

Again Jess felt disappointed at the staged nature of it all, but only for a split second. Miss Sarah, nodding curtly, returned to her previous position and with point blank precision smacked her weapon down onto the puckering velvet opening of his arse.

The mingled whine of pain and animal satisfaction that rocketed from Master Paul's mouth sent a strange shockwave through Jess. An odd feeling of chilled warmth, which intensified sharply when Mrs Peters hand unexpectedly shot up her skirt.

Jess's breath caught in her throat. Her brain was asking her why she didn't move, why she didn't knock the invading arm away, but her body was sighing with relief, telling her to stay as still as possible, silently willing her superior's hand to move up her leg to the patch of bare flesh between her stocking tops and satin panties. Jess's hands clasped the edge of the chaise longue as Mrs Peters, her eyes fixed critically on Miss Sarah, circled an individual digit around a tiny portion of nylon covered thigh.

Master Paul was given permission to stand, and as he did so Jess could see the desk top blotting paper had been employed beyond the requirements of historical accuracy, for the young man had spunked across it with the last stroke of the whip.

Miss Sarah was shaking her head at her servant's embarrassment. 'You have come already. I don't recall giving you permission.'

'No, my lady. Sorry, my lady.' His eyes remained downcast, but Jess noticed that every now and then he glanced towards his lady's breasts; a gesture Jess couldn't help copying as Mrs Peters fingers moved north, caressing the clerk's satin covered crotch, making her want to shift her position, not knowing if she should move further away, or closer. Her body told her it was bliss, her brain told her it was a woman's hand, and she didn't *do* women, and anyway, she should not be here, in this room with these strange people. *I should be filing, taking bookings. I should not be here. Not here. Not here.*

'I ought to punish you again, but His Lordship will be expecting you.' Jess realised that the session must nearly be over as Miss Sarah continued, 'However, I require your services before you return to your labours.

'Yes, my lady.' The guest's head shot up, and for the first time he stood tall, the cock that had been temporarily flaccid, stirring with new blood as he reached out with previously unseen confidence for his mistress's tits, freeing them quickly from the basque. As his mouth made contact with the neat teats, Jess shuddered, her imagination jealously interpreting how good it must feel.

'Come with me, Miss Sanders.' Mrs Peters abruptly withdrew her hand and stood up. 'I believe you have seen enough.'

Jess's mouth dropped open to protest, but her words died with the combined presence of Mrs Peters closed expression, and her own shock at how close the voyeuristic experience had taken her to coming. One touch to her clit, one squeeze of her damp knickers; that's all it would have taken. With a final glance at the servant suckling his mewling lady's chest, Jess was steered from the room towards the lift; shaken both physically and mentally.

'I believe you have work to do.' Mrs Peters' voice was completely cold.

Jess nodded dumbly, a million questions shooting around her head. *Why take me into a situation where I'm bound to get turned on and then deny me pleasure? Why take me up to the fifth floor in the first place? What was the point? I only book the sessions, nothing more.*

As the lift doors opened Jess was ushered inside. 'I hope you have learnt something from this visit, Miss Sanders.' Mrs Peters turned to walk away, but just as the doors began to close, she added, 'You are not to pleasure yourself. I'll know if you do. We have a rule here, which you'd do well to remember. You must always ask my permission before indulging in personal satisfaction.'

Jess stared at the retreating back of the manageress as the lift doors closed and she plummeted to the ground floor. Her body was desperate to come; she'd have to sneak off to the Ladies to sort herself out or she'd never get any work done. She knew Mrs Peters had told her not to, but how on earth would she find out? Jess sure as hell wasn't going to tell her.

Laura sat back in her private bedroom and switched on her laptop. She was confident of what she would see when she turned on the webcam link she'd got the barman to discreetly set up in the staff toilet cubicle first thing that morning.

Jess was already there; her skirt crunched up around her waist, her bum perched on the edge of the closed toilet lid, her back arched as an urgent finger slipped hastily back and forth over her slick nub. Her lipstick free mouth panting, her eyes shut in tight concentration, as she came with a judder of release.

'Not as innocent as she'd like to think herself.' Laura's face broke into a calculating smile. 'Some people simply can't do what they're told.'

Chapter Three

SAM WAS STANDING AT the hotel bar, almost exactly where Laura had been the night before. Although he was looking in the opposite direction, sipping from a tumbler of faintly orange liquid, Laura was sure he knew she'd entered the room.

'Are you going to finish that drink, or shall we just go to bed?'

Taken aback by her directness, Sam's eyes narrowed as he placed his barely touched drink on a nearby table and followed the manageress out of the bar, offering to carry the large canvas bag she held, saying, 'My suite I think.'

Laura raised a questioning eyebrow, but deciding it might be interesting to give him the illusion of being in control, even if only for a moment, she took a step back so Sam could lead the way to the lift.

As they walked, Sam shifted the bag from one hand to the other. 'What the hell have you got in here, it weighs a ton?'

Laura merely shrugged; he'd find out soon enough.

The second they entered the lift, Laura produced a small silver key from the palm of her hand, and punched the button that would take them to the fifth floor. As the lift began to slow towards their destination she inserted the key into the elevator's override facility and brought it to a juddering halt.

'What are you doing?' Her guest remained outwardly calm, but Laura wondered how the artist felt inside as she fixed him with a stern expression.

Despite the fact that he was the most attractive man she'd seen in months, and her own pulse was thudding rather more than she would have cared to admit, her voice remained professionally abrupt. 'Change of plan. My place instead, I think.' She tilted her head to one side, appraising him as she spoke, 'I suggest you do *exactly* what I tell you.'

Laura could almost hear the increase in Sam's heart rate, and she allowed the merest hint of a grin to waver briefly at the corner of her burgundy lips. Confident that he was too far down the road of stimulation to walk out now, and that he wouldn't leave even if he could, she calmly ordered him to remove all his clothes.

'But we're in a lift.'

Sam had merely tilted his head to one side as he'd spoken, but Laura knew from experience that her actions were beginning to unsettle him, however composed he managed to appear. Sounding like a headmistress whose patience was about to wear very thin, Laura repeated her request, 'I asked you to remove your clothes. I think you should, don't you?'

With his brown eyes clouding a little, his ever hardening erection took control of his brain, and Sam disposed of his clothes.

Not giving him the chance to think, Laura swiftly produced a pair of heavy-duty cuffs from her holdall, and secured a now openly stunned Sam's wrists behind his back. Her fingers danced briefly over the small Celtic cross tattoo on his right arm; grinning slyly at him, a plaything to her whims, his dick revealing how turned on he was, while his face showed nothing but lustful confusion.

Attired in a simple but stunning blue dress, done up at the front with nine small white buttons, Laura could feel her generous breasts pushing up inside the material, putting undue pressure on the top two fastenings.

Sam hovered apprehensively as the manageress began to rummage in her bag again. He thought back to the small business card she'd got the barman to pass on to him the night before. He'd assumed it was just one of those silly cards you could have made up in motorway service stations. Now the words, *Laura Peters; Mistress of the Fifth Floor; All needs catered for* ... had a darker meaning. Sam's eyes followed her hidden hand, his lips parting in surprise as she pulled out another set of cuffs, this time with about 30cm of linked chain connecting them. Wordlessly, she locked them around his unresisting ankles, impressed at his ability to remain silent while she made him look like an American criminal ready to shuffle dejectedly to gaol.

As Laura walked around her prisoner, she observed the thick swaying cock that just yearned to be touched, to be enveloped between her thick red lips. Snapping her eyes back to Sam's face, she smiled; he was like a captured hawk, hovering edgily to see what would happen next. The hunter had become the hunted.

'You have a hell of a hard-on there, Mr Wheeler.' Mrs Peters spoke levelly, as if she was doing no more than commenting on the state of the weather. 'It'll have to be maintained carefully or you'll spurt your load before I'm ready. OK?'

It was a question, of sorts, but Sam knew it wasn't a question that she would accept a negative response to, so he agreed. He shivered as Laura produced a black cock case. Her fingers trailed lazily around his testicles before encasing his length within the leather harness.

When he was finally restrained to her liking, Laura stood directly in front of him, her gaze piercing. 'Do you see these buttons, Sam?' She ran a manicured finger down her dress, and he nodded fervently. 'I will undo one each time I decide you deserve it. Yes?'

'Yes.' He nodded again, without really understanding what he was agreeing to, inwardly wincing at his uncharacteristically pitiable urge to do everything she asked.

'First though, I think we need a little more room to manoeuvre. Twisting the key back into position so that the lift was once again operational Laura scooped up Sam's clothes and stuffed them into her bag. Then, taking the chain that linked his handcuffs, she dragged him towards the opening doors.

Only able to shuffle within the confines of his restraints, Sam found himself dragged from the safe privacy of the lift. *What if someone sees us? Anyone could walk down this corridor at any moment.* He didn't dare complain though; just in case the sound of his voice attracted the attention of any nearby guests. The perspiration that had been threatening on his forehead, broke out in earnest as his head swung from side to side, willing each bedroom door to stay shut so that their occupants would remain unaware of his shamefully shackled yet roused state.

At last, after what seemed like an eternity to Sam, they reached Laura's quarters. She'd said nothing as they walked, but Sam had been very aware of her frequent glances towards his dick, for each time she peered at it, it leapt slightly within its bonds, making his stomach flip and his state of lust, which he'd believed to be already at its peak, grow even more urgent.

Sliding a card key into position, Laura unlocked the door and stood back so that her visitor could stumble into her compact suite. Dropping the holdall, Laura led Sam into the middle of the room. She didn't bother to hide the elation of how his submission delighted her. The expression of bewildered craving on his face did more for her personal arousal than he would ever understand. How she loved taking control of powerful men.

Let's make it easy to start with, shall we,' Laura took a step forwards, 'kneel down and tell me who you are.'

Her voice was calm again now and Sam was relieved to be able to obey so easily, although kneeling was harder than expected within the constrictions of his bonds. Once he'd managed to position himself successfully he recited his full name, 'Samuel Wheeler.'

Laura rewarded him with an opened button, grinning wickedly as Sam's face showed how cheated he felt that she'd started from unfastening the bottom of her dress, rather than instantly freeing her luscious tits. He opened his mouth to say something; anything to try and regain some control, some pride, but one glance at Laura's face stopped him. She was furious. Livid. But he had no idea why. Sam's body quelled and he found he was cowering before her.

Thrilled at having made him feel so small so quickly with her fake anger, Laura spoke sharply, 'Lie face down on the floor.'

Sam hesitated, and she barked out 'Do it!'

Stumbling forward onto his face, unable to stop the involuntary shaking in his shoulders, Sam didn't see his tormentor take the paddle out of her bag, but became all too aware of it, when three sharp blows hit his backside with swift accuracy.

As she struck, the threatening swish of the paddle echoing its continual potential for pain as it arched through the air, Laura shouted, 'Who are you? What are you?'

Sam thought he'd been panicking before, but that was nothing to what he felt now. Genuine alarm swept through him as he struggled to understand what she meant.

Laura dropped her weapon to the floor, and dragged Sam back to his feet. He swayed as he watched her open a second tiny white button. His arse smarted, and the glut of ruby splodges that broke out across his chest as he was ordered to kneel again, showed Laura how close the artist was to climax. Stepping as near to him as possible without making bodily contact, the swaying fabric of the partially opened dress caressing his face, Laura locked her eyes on to Sam's. Stealthily she lifted the flaps of her dress wider so he could see she wore no underwear beneath. Sam was so close to her sex he could smell it. If she hadn't ordered him to lick her clit he knew he would have risked her anger and done it anyway.

Lapping at Laura's delicious sticky juice, he smeared her private liquid around his parched lips, flicking her nub with the very end of his tongue. Sam couldn't imagine how she remained so controlled, for just as he was getting ready to push her on into a climax the manageress took a step back and, without giving him any indication if she had enjoyed his attention or not, she undid another button. 'You will tell me who you are, and what you are, or you will not be allowed to do that again.'

Sam stared at her in disbelief. She was making no sense. How could the woman be so cold, how could denying herself pleasure be a way to get at him? Somehow it was, though, and he already missed her taste. Speaking with as much conviction as he could muster he said, 'My name is Sam Wheeler and I'm an artist.'

'And?' She picked the paddle back up and struck his left nipple. Hard.

Tears sprang to his eyes as pain shot through his flesh. He flinched as the paddle connected with expert accuracy against his other nipple. *Who the hell is this woman?*

Mrs Peters undid another button. Sam moistened his lips, his need to see her completely naked growing out of all proportion as his cock strained within its case, liquid dribbling from its tip. Keeping hold of the paddle, she told him to bend over. His hands and knees scuffed against the rough carpet as he braced himself for Laura to ask his name again, but was caught off guard when she asked who he worked for instead.

'Myself,' Sam said quickly. Too quickly perhaps, for the thin white paddle cracked down on his exposed rump before the word had completely left his lips. After four strikes, she pulled him back up, rewarding him for withstanding the pain with another button. That was five open now, and her strong shapely legs were on show. Somehow the agony she was inflicting wasn't as bad as having to wait so long for her continued unbuttoning.

'It's time for us to get serious.' Laura rolled Sam onto his back, and, with his hands trapped beneath him and his dick sticking up like a black flag pole, she lifted her dress and sat astride his legs, the cock holder rubbing against her flawless round stomach.

'We'll begin again. So, who are you? And don't give me any of that Sam Wheeler crap. You know what I want to hear.'

'I don't know what you're talking about.' The pleading words were coming automatically now, as Laura began to rock back and forth, her wetness trickling over his trapped skin.

'Your role in life?'

The droplets that spotted his brow morphed into full blown sweat as he answered her, his voice barely a whisper, 'An artist.'

'No. Not *just* an artist.' Slim fingers went to the top of her dress. Laura's tone was soft now, and suddenly she was back into seducing territory. 'If you tell me, I'll undo this button. You'd like me to, wouldn't you?'

It was only a button. A single small white disc, but it was holding back so much promise, and he wanted to see that chest so badly. The artist blurted out, 'I don't understand what you want me to say.'

Warm palms came forward and soothed Sam's sticky brow. Laura spoke as if reassuring a naughty child, 'Now now, you're a clever man. Think a while. What are you?'

Sam's throat turned from simply dry to sandpaper rough, and suddenly he understood what she wanted. The realisation was worse than not knowing.

The tension in the room multiplied as her dress flapped against him. As he gazed at the manageress, she ran both hands up inside the blue material, circling sharp fingertips around her nipples. Although unable to see exactly what she was doing, Sam could tell how excited she was. The tips of her breasts poked harder than ever through the cotton and the mewl that escaped her lips as she worked herself off showed him that Laura Peters was human after all.

As she continued to rock against Sam's aching legs, Laura asked him again, her digits still working on her own stimulation. 'Tell me, I know you've worked it out. Tell me, or you'll never see just how desperate my tits are for you right now.'

'I can't … I …' Sam's pride laboured to assert itself as Laura moved faster.

He yowled, his crushed hands were becoming more squashed by the second, and his limbs began to go numb beneath her weight. Yet, through all this his cock remained taut, and not just because of its leather guardian. Sam was so hard for Laura he was amazed his shaft didn't burst out of its tiny prison all on its own.

Abruptly, the woman rose and undid another button, properly revealing her soft fluffy pussy and smooth stomach. Only three buttons remained now, and Sam's mind jumped ahead to the final result, conveniently skipping what he might have to endure to get to that point unless he told Mrs Peters what she wanted to hear.

She was running her blood red fingernails around her navel as she continued to question him. 'Let's try again. Who do you work for?'

'Myself.' Laura shook her head sadly, and going to a small wooden box on her bookshelf, produced two silver nipple clamps. Without giving Sam time to prepare for the coming sting, she deftly clipped them onto his chest.

He bit his lips together to try and deflect the icy agony, while his body attempted to adjust to its latest torture. Twirling the cruel toys back and forth, she sent fresh shocks of pain through him. Speaking through clenched teeth, Laura repeated, 'Who-do-you-work-for?'

It was too much. Everything ached. Everything hurt. He shouted into the expectant hush of the room, 'You.'

'At last!' With a relief at his capitulation greater than she'd anticipated, Laura removed the clamps and placed her hot sensuous lips against the scarred tissue, kissing life back into his flesh. 'You see how nice it can feel to tell the truth?'

Sam didn't speak, his dick moved within its casing; a wave or precome trickling down the leather.

Laura undid another button. Only two remained

fastened now. The vital two that held back her chest. She manoeuvred Sam gently to his feet. It took a while to steady his footing as the artist's abused body swam in an ungainly fashion.

'You should start telling me a bit more of the truth if you ever want to come. Unless of course,' she stroked a finger along the length of his shaft, 'you want to stay encased for ever.'

Sam blinked at her, not knowing what to say, but embarrassingly aware that the last vestiges of his resolve were crumbling.

'When you say that you are mine again, I'm going to take off that harness, and then I'm going to lick your balls until you explode. After that ...' Laura's erratic voice lowered to a seductive whisper, '... I'm going to undo the rest of my buttons and you can see my tits, kiss them, hide your face in them, lick them again and again until your cock is hot. Then you can impale me on it, make me squirm, make me scream ...'

Sam barely heard what she said. All he could see was the vision she was creating, and sinking to his knees in defeat, knowing she'd been the victor from the second they'd walked into the lift, he bellowed into the small room. 'I work for you!'

Laura's triumphant face said it all. Crouching before him, her stumbling fingers showed just how much she'd been getting off on her authority over him.

With the case removed, Sam felt a strange mixture of relief, failure and heavy eroticism flood him, as the mistress engulfed his balls in her mouth, lapping until he creamed the carpet with an explosion of spunk.

Undoing the remaining little white buttons, Laura slipped her dress from her shoulders. Finally, blessedly naked, she was all Sam had imagined. Exhausted and meek before her, he mentally worshipped her, silently pleading to be allowed to touch her sun-enhanced skin, bury himself between her breasts, and fuck her senseless.

Sitting on the edge of her bed, Laura considered the man before her. 'New territory for you I suspect, letting a woman take the upper hand? You did want to shag me though.'

He sounded hoarse as he replied, 'It certainly was very different.'

Sam coughed as Laura's eyes shone with victory. Her body, though still outwardly controlled, was desperate for some attention of its own. About to make a move to satisfy her own desires, Laura's eyebrows rose with surprise as Sam continued, 'I wanted to seduce you with flowers and champagne, make love to you slowly, lingeringly, and explore every inch of you.' He couldn't say any more, he felt foolish and exposed, and his throat rasped from the effort of speech.

'I'm not sure about that romantic crap, but the champagne bit sounds good,' Laura went to the mini-fridge in the corner of the room.

Sam watched as she grasped the bottle, popped the cork with little fuss, and poured two brimming glasses of bubbly. He could taste it even before Laura brought the blissfully cold liquid to his lips.

After helping him take a few gulps, Laura's domineering stance relaxed a little. 'Do you promise to be a good boy if I undo your wrists?'

'I promise.' Unclipping him, Laura rubbed some life back into Sam's cramped muscles before passing him a drink. Knocking the entire glassful back in one deep draft, Sam never took his eyes off her chest.

'More?' Laura passed him the bottle without waiting for a reply.

Refilling his glass, the artist glugged back the golden juice. The second the last drop of alcohol hit the back of his neck, something in Sam snapped. He couldn't wait any longer; his patience and the suppression of his natural dominance had been stretched to the limit. Putting down the glass and stumbling forward in his ankle cuffs, he lunged at Laura Peters, clasping his teeth around her left breast. She yelped with animal delight as he nipped her skin. Holding a tit in each palm, Sam nuzzled her luminous flesh, gorging himself on the objects of his tortured arousal, until, with a swift half smile, Laura said, with incredible composure, 'You may fuck me now, slave, but only because I want you to. Next time there will be stricter rules.'

Chapter Four

ALTHOUGH A NIGHT HAD passed since her surreal encounter on the fifth floor, Jess still felt an involuntary twitch between her legs each time she thought about it.

Her efforts to put it to the back of her mind were thwarted by Mrs Peters, who'd been continually popping in and out of the reception and booking office area that morning.

With each of her visits, an increasing unease stole over Jess. She knew the older woman had been watching her. The accusatory expression that crossed her employer's face whenever they met, instantly made Jess feel guilty for her body's reaction to the bizarre experience. The private knowledge that she'd physically enjoyed the abuse of another human being, however much they had welcomed it, was also proving hard to deal with, and had left Jess feeling ashamed and humiliated. A humiliation she was determined never to admit to, at least, not out loud.

As her desk clock struck 10 a.m. the dominating presence of Mrs Peters loomed once again outside the office, beckoning to Jess with a single elongated finger. As the clerk rose from her seat and went to the manageress's side, her palms immediately became clammy.

Jess said nothing as they walked; she was too busy

trying to stamp out the voice that was shouting at the back of her head, telling her to get out and never look back, as a simultaneous stab of erotic anticipation ripped through her body at the thought of observing more of the activities that took place on the fifth floor.

Since her enforced visit to the study Jess had taken a couple of bookings for Fables' private rooms, and her mind had built up a picture of each of the so far unseen locations with frequent and detailed repetition. Jess had told no one what had happened in the Victorian study. There was no one to tell. She worked alone in her little office, and the reception staff, who came and went after every few hours, had little opportunity to chat or exchange more than a smile of greeting between customers and phone calls. Nor was there anyone at home in Jess's poky flat near Oxford's busy railway station. There hadn't been anyone special in Jess's life for a long time, and even when there had been, it had always been strictly straight sex, nothing kinky, nothing unusual, nothing rough, and certainly nothing involving women. She'd never even considered it.

The quiet hum of the lift was almost unbearable as they began their ascent to the fifth floor. Jess, who could normally happily ignore such silences, started to burble about how good business had been this week, but the verbal outpouring froze on her lips when Mrs Peters nailed her with a cold stare, and for the remainder of the mercifully short trip she mutely fiddled with the folds of her pleated skirt.

Only a few steps down the corridor from the lift, they reached a solid wooden door adorned with the number 52. Mrs Peters addressed Jess, 'Room 52 is a rather different place to the study you visited, Miss Sanders, but I'm sure you'll enjoy it just as much. More perhaps.'

Pushing the door open, Jess, painfully conscious of her heightened state of anxiety, was ushered inside. Quickly, she surveyed her surroundings. A school room. Not copied from some ancient dusty Victorian or Edwardian school house, but a modern classroom with plastic-topped stainless steel-legged tables and chairs, and a computerised white board, rather than a blackboard.

As Jess hesitated next to a shelf unit holding pencils, pens, rulers and associated school equipment, she risked her first proper glance of the day at her boss. She was looking straight at her.

'Sit down.' Mrs Peters pulled out a small grey plastic seat, and Jess obeyed, glad to be able to hide the nervous shake that had started in her legs.

Once seated, Jess's knees bent up on the infant-sized furniture, Mrs Peters returned to the classroom door, and, without waiting for anyone else to enter, bolted it. Jess immediately stood up in alarm. Her mouth opened to protest, but once again the expression on her superior's face dissolved the words before they had left her throat.

In two swift strides the manageress stood over Jess. She tried to push the seat back a bit, but Mrs Peters had chosen where to place her well and the clerk found herself trapped between her boss and a large art table. Mrs Peters' hard jade eyes flashed. 'I think it best you stay where you are for a moment.'

Jess stared back at her for a split second, lowering her gaze in embarrassment at the effect the taller woman's proximity was having on her pulse rate. She stared at her employer's black kitten-heeled shoes, the hem of her black suit trousers, the flash of naked ankle; anything not to see the calculating knowing look on Mrs Peters' face.

While Jess was focusing her attention elsewhere, Mrs Peters took advantage and, produced a short silk rope from her jacket pocket. Before the clerk knew what was happening, her arms had been wrenched behind her back. She gasped in surprise as the tether was pulled taut and deftly looped through the gap in the back of the chair.

Her face devoid of emotion, Mrs Peters gave the bindings a quick tug to make sure they were secure and then retreated to the other side of the room, and, without a backward glance, opened the door to a walk-in cupboard, and stepped inside.

What the hell was she doing? Jess wriggled against the bonds. No one had ever tied her up before. She felt trapped, frightened, and yet, she could already feel the treacherous awakening of her body. Every second of the wait felt like a lifetime as Jess speculated on what might happen next. She could so clearly picture the beating Master Paul had received. *Was that going to happen to her?* As she thought about it, her nipples hardened; poking against the cotton bra she wore beneath her black blouse.

The cupboard re-opened, and Jess sucked in a shocked breath as she saw Mrs Peters emerge. Wearing a silk copy of an antiquated teachers robe around her shoulders, and brandishing a long thin hooked school cane in her hand, she approached Jess. The clerk was transfixed by the sight; made more striking by it being so out of place in the otherwise modern room.

Although the gown reached most of the way around Mrs Peters' body, enough of a gap existed to show she wore nothing beneath, and suddenly Jess understood the attraction that both her boss and this room would hold for the various paying guests that came its way.

Jess knew she should run. Despite her restrained arms, she could stand, and even with the small chair strapped to her like a tortoise's shell, she could still make a dash to the door. It was just an ordinary bolt; and her fingers had enough manoeuvrability to slide it back. She could be out of the room in seconds, leave the Fables Hotel and go back to temping. No one would care. But she didn't move. Jess just sat there, her eyes glued to the chink of body on view, the creamy round firm stomach, the fluff of chestnut pussy that matched Mrs Peters professionally trussed mane of hair, the briefest glimpse of rounded tit as she walked nearer to Jess, the gown billowing teasingly around her nakedness.

Peering over the top of a pair of exquisite fake glasses, Mrs Peters looked every bit the cross teacher. Her eyes twinkled with malevolent satisfaction as she regarded the clerk. Taking the end of the hooked cane, Laura Peters flicked the girl's hair from her forehead, and with a firm pressure, tilted her head back so Jess was forced to meet her gaze. 'Do you know why you are here?'

Jess shook her head as Mrs Peters perched against the table opposite her, all the time caressing and stroking the cane as if it were a favoured pet. Jess tried hard to think, but all she could focus on was the rope around her wrists, the glimpse of tempting nakedness this strange woman afforded her, and the presence of the cane.

'I'm beginning to think you like my company.'

'I …' Jess didn't have a chance to continue.

An uncompromising tone of clipped bluntness issued from the manageress's lips. 'You are here to be punished.'

'Punished? But why?' Jess thought hastily back over the last week. She was sure she hadn't made any mistakes with the bookings. In fact Mr Davies had praised her only that morning for her swift understanding of the hotel's workings.

Trailing the cane down Jess's neck, Mrs Peters went

40

on, 'Can you really think of nothing? Of no act of disobedience?'

Jess, her eyes still transfixed by the cane, shook her head.

'I see.' Turning away from her mock-pupil, Mrs Peters began to search the equipment shelf.

Aware of the frantic increase in her heart rate, Jess took some deep breaths, and tried to calm down. She couldn't remember breaking any rules. Unless becoming unwillingly turned on while watching Miss Sarah and Master Paul counted. *It couldn't have been that though, surely? That was what Mrs Peters had wanted. Wasn't it?*

Again confusion swamped Jess as she tried to work out the rules to a game she hadn't even asked to play. As she saw Mrs Peters placing something into her gown pocket, her attempts to remain calm dissolved further and panic nudged her brain. *What the hell was she so keen to hide?*

'You've had time to consider your situation, Miss Sanders. Now tell me, why do you need to be punished?'

Shaking her head, Jess replied meekly, 'I don't know, Mrs Peters. I'm sorry.'

'You are wise to be sorry, girl, but in this establishment, sorry isn't enough. Punishment is the real method of education, don't you think?'

Jess almost said that, no she didn't, but thought better of it and said, 'Yes of course.'

Mrs Peters' voice was sickly sweet as she pulled the concealed object from her pocket.

'How fortunate that you agree with me, Miss Sanders. That in itself will save you from some level of discomfort.' Sweat dotted the back of Jess's neck as she observed the shiny silver scissors. These were not the blunt ended tools that she associated with classrooms, but sharp dressmaker's scissors. Jess shrunk back as far as the mini chair would allow.

An almost demonic smile of satisfaction on her face, Mrs Peters stooped down, the gown opening around her, giving Jess a strikingly distracting view as her eyes darted from her employer's firm tits, to the scissors, and back again in swift repetition.

'I'd keep very still if I were you.'

A nagging voice at the back of Jess's mind wondered why she wasn't protesting, but no words came as she watched, mesmerised. The artificial light of the room reflected against the blades as they got closer and closer.

It wasn't until Mrs Peters grabbed the bottom of her blouse and slid the material between the shimmering blades that Jess's brain finally accepted what was about to happen. As the first snip of fabric was made Jess cried out in protest, but the proximity of the scissors made her whole body freeze rather than pull away. With concentrated determination Mrs Peters continued to cut open her clerk's top. Jess threw her head back as the cutting edge inched up towards the neck line, the cold metal teasing her warm flesh, the scissors making short work of destroying her top.

As the air conditioning caressed her newly revealed skin, Mrs Peters snipped the remaining material from Jess's torso, leaving her in her skirt, knickers and white cotton bra, her breasts pushing upwards as they began to feel unbearably constrained.

From somewhere deep within her, Jess found her voice, 'How dare you! That was my favourite T-shirt. I ...' The uncharacteristic bravery caused by her indignation died on her tongue as Mrs Peters twisted the ruined top into shape, and thrust it between Jess's teeth, gagging her with an expert ease.

Shocked, Jess tried to shout into the cloth, but her

words were muffled, and the realisation that her outburst was only serving to delight her boss further made her quieten down and drop her chin.

'That's better, Miss Sanders.' Mrs Peters crouched in front of her pupil, placing her cool hands on Jess's knees. 'I would have preferred not to have to silence you, but obviously I can't yet trust you to keep your feelings to yourself. This is something you will learn to do in time.'

Jess listened to the words, trying to make sense of them. This was not what she was here for. She was just the administrative girl for goodness' sake.

Mrs Peters pulled at the white cotton bra, and Jess's breasts popped into view. Jess bit her lips to hold back the unwilling sigh of satisfaction that their release brought to her throat. 'Beautiful tits, Miss Sanders. You are truly blessed. Above average size and yet firm. Many would pay for such a chest as this.'

Jess wouldn't have replied even if she could. She knew her chest was her best feature, but felt no pleasure in Mrs Peters compliments.

'I wonder how badly you want me to kiss your nipples, how much you want me to hold them between my fingers?'

The clerk knew she was blushing, knew that the dampness between her legs was directly in response to her superior's words, and suddenly she was grateful for the gag. Grateful she was unable to reply, for any denial of her desire for those things would be a lie, and Jess was a rotten liar.

Mrs Peters took hold of the back of Jess's short red hair and yanked it hard, so that she had no choice but to look at her captor. Then Mrs Peters picked up her cane and rubbed it against the very tip of Jess's right nipple, making her gasp at the sensations that the thin wand shot through her chest. 'Is that nice, Miss Sanders?'

Jess bit hard into the remains of her T-shirt, her eyes squeezed shut, trying not to show anything on her face except defiance. Mrs Peters merely laughed, and moved the cane to the other teat. Tears gathered at the corner of Jess's eyes, but she angrily willed them away, trying to think of her spreadsheets, of the pile of washing up she'd left in the kitchen sink that morning, anything other than the fantastic but contradictory feelings that surged through her.

'Are you listening to me, Jess?'

The use of her first name broke Jess's concentration for a second and she nodded.

'Good. Now, I want to you to tell me the truth. Did you, or did you not pleasure yourself after seeing Miss Sarah and Master Paul together last week, even though I expressly told you not to?'

At last Jess understood why she was being chastised, but how had Mrs Peters found out? *She can't really read minds, can she?* Jess blinked, unsure how to react. *Would it be better to confess or to deny?*

'I see you aren't so stupid as to deny it, you have at least the sense to think it through.' Mrs Peters began to flex the cane between her palms, making Jess gulp behind her gag. 'You did, didn't you?'

Jess sat, statue still, fear knotting her stomach as she watched the cane move, listening to the mild buzz it made as Mrs Peters swiped it, cutting the air.

'Last time of asking, Miss Sanders.'

Strangely, Jess felt better now Mrs Peters had reverted to using her surname and almost imperceptibly she inclined her head.

The cane was lowered straight away and Mrs Peters grabbed Jess's jaw between her fingers, forcing her to confront her piercing eyes. 'You are very wise. You see, I know that you wanked off afterwards. I heard. I saw.'

Jess's mind whirled, *how on earth?*

The manageress stood upright, giving Jess another flash of her curvaceous body. 'You are speculating how I know, how I saw and heard you gasp and groan while you ran a damp finger over your nub in a hurried visit to the ladies' lavatory.'

If her jaw could have fallen open it would have done; as it was Jess dribbled dumbly into the ruin of her T-shirt.

'You see, I have a few mobile cameras placed here and there. They prove very useful.' Mrs Peters seemed to think for a moment as if undecided, and then, reverting to type, brought the cane down hard onto Jess's right tit.

The gag wasn't sufficient to disguise Jess's scream. Tears of shocked anguish streamed down her cheeks as the sting lingered long after the cane had left her tender flesh. Then Mrs Peters bent down and kissed the wounded tit. Jess couldn't believe how fantastic it felt as her boss's moist lips soothed the stung flesh.

When the cane struck her left side, Jess was already riding out the pain, and waiting on the blissful kiss that she hoped would follow. Mrs Peters quickly obliged, before drawing back, and slipping the gown from her shoulders. The groan that escaped from Jess's mouth at the glorious sight was lost, but the lust driven look on her face spoke volumes to her boss who privately congratulated herself that, once again, her instincts were spot on. Jess Sanders was born for this life.

'That was your punishment. I trust you understand how lightly you have been let off. Such direct disobedience normally carries a much stiffer penalty. However, there is another matter we need to discuss.'

Another matter? Jess, her breasts still smarting, her clit slick from the strange unfamiliar mixture of terror and eroticism that swam through her veins, couldn't even begin to think what the other "matter" might be. She shifted a little against the plastic seat. Her legs unbearably hot in the long skirt, and her cotton knickers stuck to her with the suction of her own juices.

'I see you are uncomfortable. Don't worry, Miss Sanders, as soon as you've answered my next question satisfactorily, I will relieve your condition.'

Jess's flesh inflamed further. She knew perfectly well what Mrs Peters meant this time. If she told the manageress what she wanted to hear she would be allowed to come, if she didn't … well, Jess didn't want to think about that.

Picking up the silk gown, Mrs Peters rotated a small section of the smooth material over Jess's breasts. Over and around the delicate undersides, across the pert nipples, the pseudo-schoolteacher kept up a firm pressure against her pupil's chest.

A gush of liquid escaped from between Jess's legs and her body shock as the fist signs of a forthcoming climax began to simmer like trapped bubbles in her stomach.

Mrs Peters smiled her semi-sadistic smile and, knowing full well how desperate Jess was to come, said, 'Think, child. Think carefully. Were you turned on by watching Master Paul, and were you, as I suspect, jealous of him? Did you wish that it was you leaning across that desk and not him? I think you did. I think you wished that very much indeed.'

Jealous? The thought hadn't entered Jess's mind, but now, as Mrs Peters kept up the delicious pressure against her right nipple, she could see that it was true. It was obvious. She *had* been jealous, she *had* wondered what it would be like, but now she was here, did she really want to know? And more importantly, what were the consequences of her admitting as much to Mrs Peters?

Jess shook her head vehemently.

The sigh Mrs Peters gave was as much of pleasure as of disappointment, pleasure that she could continue the torture she was evidently enjoying so much.

It didn't matter if Jess closed her eyes or not now, she could still see the vision of her tormentor's voluptuously shapely body. It seemed to have become imprinted on her retina. As Mrs Peters repeated her question, the gown was pressed a little harder against the clerk's soft globes, and Jess felt tension ripple across her shoulders, as she was visited by another new realisation. She desperately, wanted to suck on the breasts that hung so invitingly before her. The desire to take one of her superior's nipples between her teeth and roll it around her tongue was almost overwhelming.

A hard slap connected with her left teat, and the tears that had been prickling at the corners of Jess's eyes broke out with the shock of new agony.

'This is very unwise of you, Miss Sanders, you must realise I could keep you like this all day. Keep you on the brink of ecstasy, without letting you dip even a toe over the edge.'

Gasping for breath into the now soggy gag, Jess knew her body was beginning to betray her. She tried to concentrate, focusing on the shelf on the wall, counting the pots of pens and pencils, anything not to think about that other body, her own body, and how badly she needed to feel them come next to each other.

Following the line of Jess's stare, Mrs Peters moved back, making Jess mentally howl with loss as she dropped the silk gown, and went to the shelf to collect a pencil.

'I will ask you one more time, Miss Sanders.'

Kneeling, the pseudo-teacher pushed Jess's legs as wide open as they would go, and then, easing the damp panties to one side, began to tease the blunt end of the pencil around, but not on, her engorged clit. All the time she watched Jess's face, fully aware that there wasn't much fight left in her now. 'Were you jealous of him, child?'

Clamping her jaw, Jess shut her eyes tighter, but all that did was intensify the sparks of need that the pencil was providing as it slid around in her juice, not quite touching her need, not quite disappearing up inside her gaping hole.

'When you tell me the truth I am going to slide this pencil inside you, then I'm going to let you lick my tits, and I'll untie you, and give you what you want most of all. An orgasm so strong, that you'll never forget it in the whole of your life.'

It was too much. The picture her boss had painted was so clear to Jess. She could almost feel all of those things happening. All she had to do was say she was jealous. What would it hurt now? She was far too far down the road of desire to turn back, and there was no way she'd escape if she didn't say it.

Gritting her teeth, Jess looked down, and with a small sigh of despaired lust, inclined her head.

Mrs Peters said nothing, but the speed with which she moved spoke volumes. Jess was untied, and her gag removed as she was dragged to her shaking unsteady feet. Her skirt and knickers were whipped away before she'd even registered the fact, and then, the teasing pencil was rubbed wonderfully hard over her clit, while a large firm tit was proffered to her dry mouth.

Instinct took over, and from somewhere deep within her, Jess knew exactly what to do, sucking and lapping at the breast, as the frustratingly thin pencil was eased in and out of her pussy with tantalising regularity

Just as she was about to come, Mrs Peters pulled back and flipped Jess over, so she was lying face down on one of the tables, her legs dangling to the ground, her bum the perfect target for the cane, which now came down on her with ferocious speed. Jess screamed as lash after lash connected with her virgin arse. As she held onto the table, her knuckles turning white her mind raced. *Had she really wanted this?* Yet, even as she thought it, Jess was wondering what her arse looked like. *Is it covered in pretty pink lines and lash marks like Paul's was?*

The burning sensation that shot through her skin began to change, turning into a distant tingle, a hot urgent ache that she didn't want to end. As Mrs Peters left longer and longer gaps between her strikes Jess found herself talking as if from far away, begging her not to stop, not to ever stop. It was as if the words were coming from someone else's throat, not her own.

Then Mrs Peters dropped her cane, and roughly rolling the clerk onto her back, brought her lips to her clit. Jess spasmed and cried out like she'd never done before. Her whole being involved in her climax, every nerve, every muscle, from her toes to the tingling top of her head.

When she eventually stopped quivering, naked and crumpled in a heap on the classroom floor, Jess dared a shamefaced look at the manageress.

Mrs Peters was staring down at her employee, her hands on her hips. There was no victory on her face. That, she carefully hid away. An expression of total disdain and indifference met Jess, a look that made her feel cold and utterly worthless, as though she'd failed.

'Look at the state of you child. Stand up!'

Jess, her head still swimming, was too disorientated to do anything but obey as she found herself steered to a large art table.

'Lie face down on that.'

Again Jess obeyed, her body still shaking with the aftermath of her orgasm as Mrs Peters produced four lengths of rope and deftly secured her wrists and ankles to each table leg. Grabbing a thick handled paintbrush from the room's art supplies, she flashed it before Jess's startled face, before plunging it firmly between the clerk's open legs, plugging her pussy to the hilt.

Vaguely aware of a phone beeping, Jess looked around as best she could. Mrs Peters was reading a message on her mobile, smug satisfaction on her face. Without giving Jess time to speak, she swept back into the cupboard, dressed, and headed to the door saying, 'Do not move – not that you can. I'll finish with you later.' And with that, she left.

Chapter Five

SAM WASN'T QUITE SURE why he was still there. His bag had been packed for over an hour, and there was nothing to stop him from leaving the hotel and heading back to the flat in Oxford, which doubled as both his home and his studio. He looked at his watch. There was still two hours until he had to check out of the room.

He hadn't slept well. It had been incredibly late by the time he'd been allowed to return to his own bed, and he'd been so high on the experiences of the evening before, that relaxing enough to drift off had been nigh on impossible.

There was no denying that Laura Peters had unsettled him. No woman had ever dominated Sam before. That was his role. The artist would have been disgusted with himself, except there was no disguising how fantastic it had felt – in the end. Had that made up for the initial humiliation, the shame of being shackled and dragged along a public corridor? He knew it was only sheer luck that had prevented anyone other than Laura from seeing him in that state.

Sam tried to remember what Laura had said to him. Something about there being stricter rules *next time*. Had she even mentioned meeting tomorrow? Well, it was tomorrow now, so did he just leave, should he try and find her first? She was probably at work anyway, and when he stopped to consider what kind of work she did, Sam wasn't sure he wanted to see her again anyway.

At the same time he didn't want to just disappear either. He couldn't stop thinking of that succulent body, those tits, those hypnotising green eyes. There was no doubt in his mind that Laura Peters was bad news. Sadistic, manipulative, cruel even, but she was also the most beautiful creature he'd even seen. He had to do something, he had to … His eyes fell on his case of artist's materials.

Picking up his sketchbook, Sam selected some charcoal, and began to draw; bold, thick, curvaceous, strokes that covered the page. Shutting his eyes as he worked, the image of Laura propped against the bar was etched precisely from his subconscious to the page.

He smoothed, drew, smudged, adjusted and perfected lines of black and grey until, an hour later, there she was, Laura, immortalised on the hitherto white page. Tracing a finger over the image he'd produced, Sam could almost feel the ripple of naked flesh through the fabric of her dress. The lust he'd experienced in the quiet of his sleepless night returned as he caressed the picture, smearing some of the loose charcoal dust under light fingertips.

His dick stirred within his suit, and, as he continued to touch the paper, it hardened into a thick rod. Slipping his trousers down, his eyes fixed on the drawing, Sam teased a hand over the bulge of his cotton briefs, pretending it was Laura's touch and not his own that caused his cock to jump within its confinement.

Rolling down his underwear, Sam felt the satisfying spring of his cock as it leapt free, pointing towards the drawing of Laura accusingly. Wrapping a fist around his shaft, he began pumping backwards and forwards, while his other hand strayed amongst the small shock of hair that surrounded his testicles. Sam tangled and teased his fingers through each curl, as he hoped Laura would do again.

Mentally disciplining himself, he kept his movements steady until flecks of white moisture began to gather at his tip. With a huge effort of will Sam ran from the sketch to the bathroom, violently shooting his load into the shower tray.

As he cleaned himself up he took a deep breath. He wanted her too much. She was dangerous. He would leave. He would go now.

Laura had been expecting the message. All the time she had been with Miss Sanders in the school room, she'd been listening for the buzz of her mobile. Having instructed Lee to man the reception desk, she primed him to contact her the moment a Mr Samuel Wheeler came to check out.

Abandoning the clerk, Laura hastened towards Reception. She was just in time to see Sam hand a package over to Lee, who looked visibly relieved to see his superior arrive. No doubt, Laura thought to herself, he had been running out of plausible reasons to delay Mr Wheeler's departure as he'd been instructed.

Instinct told her to pull back, to wait, and so she hovered at a distance, giving a barely discernable nod of her head towards Lee, who bid a relieved and polite goodbye to their guest. Only after Sam had exited through the large wooden double front door, did Laura hasten towards the desk.

'He left a package for you, Mrs Peters.' Lee spoke hesitantly, unsure if his task had been completed successfully or not, fully aware of the consequences of failure.

'Thank you.' Laura reached out an elegant hand to receive the A4 padded envelope. Turning it over in her hands she took it into her private office and eased open the seal, surprised to find her heart beating with rather less cool reserve than usual.

Wrapped in both thick tissue and a layer of protective tracing paper, Laura expelled a large intake of breath as she drew out the unframed sketch. It was a flawless piece of work, and like Sam before her, she found herself caressing the pencil lines of her back, her hip and her chest, taking care not to smudge her picture.

As she handled the paper, her fingers became aware of something taped to its back. Her instinct to hang back had been correct. A broad knowing smile crossed Laura's face as she found Sam's business card. Gently peeling it away from the paper, Laura placed it into her pocket. It didn't matter that the hotel computer held all his contact details. This would make it easier, as he obviously wanted her to call him. Naturally she'd make him wait though until she judged the time was absolutely right.

Taking another long look at the picture, registering how much pent up emotion had been part of its creation, Laura slid it back into the envelope and locked it in her desk, before readopting her usual stern persona, confident that no one had seen her moment of personal delight and her secret smile of satisfaction.

Her mother had always told her to trust her instincts. This week, with the arrival of both Jess and Sam into her life, they seemed to be working to perfection. Feeling particularly pleased with herself, Laura Peters retraced her steps towards the fifth floor. It was time to check on the progress of Miss Sanders.

*　　*　　*

The school clock, placed high up on the wall to Jess's right hand side, had a loud taunting tick. As each second went by Jess's indignation at having been trussed and then left had turned to annoyance and anger and then moved hurriedly on to fear. *How much longer am I going to be left like this? What's going to happen next?*

The muscles in her arms and legs ached from lack of movement, and, as Jess wriggled her body in a pointless attempt to get comfortable, the tethers at her ankles and wrists dug deeper into her pale skin. The paintbrush, wedged so tightly in her wet channel, sent frequent waves of longing through her cruelly abandoned body.

When was Mrs Peters coming back? Where had she gone? Jess thought about the work she was supposed to be doing. *Would Mr Davies be cross with her? Surely he must know what Mrs Peters was doing?* The idea that others knew of her humiliation made Jess feel worse still as she lay against the unyielding surface with nothing to do but let her imagination run away with her.

When it finally came, the sound of the door opening took Jess by surprise. She had been drifting into an uncomfortable doze, when she was abruptly brought back to attention. Craning her neck as far up as possible, Jess saw Mrs Peters striding towards her, a look of victory playing at the corner of her lips.

'You have a visitor, Miss Sanders.' Laura ushered Lee forward. 'This is Master Philips, but you may call him Lee.'

Jess coloured violently as she observed the young man's eyes stray over her naked body. Recognising him as the barman and general dogsbody, Jess noticed how different he seemed as he stood in Mrs Peters' shadow. The confident persona he presented to the hotels guests was gone, and instead she saw a meek man with a lowered head, who hovered behind their boss.

'Master Philips, this is Miss Jess Sanders, the new administration clerk, and soon, well ... let's just say, I have high hopes for this young lady.'

Jess's brain galloped off at a number of conflicting tangents as Lee nodded in evident understanding. An understanding Jess certainly did not share. *What high hopes?*

'While you were lying here enjoying yourself, Miss Sanders, Master Philips here, has proffered me a great service.'

Jess said nothing, her eyes trained on the white tabletop before her, not wanting to see the predatory look of either of the people who towered over her. She could feel the sexual tension rising in the stale air of the room, and her body tingled.

Daring another glance at the young man, Jess took in the short dark hair, the slim body, the midnight blue eyes, and the unmistakable bulge of a hard cock beneath his suit trousers, which made her pussy give an involuntary spasm against the brush.

'As you can see, Master Philip, Miss Sanders has been corked with one of the heftier classrooms paintbrushes. Just a little something to keep that untutored body amused in my absence.'

Jess closed her eyes as she heard Mrs Peters talking about her as if she was a mere thing, a toy to be played with. The idea appalled her, and yet, somehow the thought that they could do whatever they liked to her, sent another shot of desire through her abused frame, confusing her further.

Lee said nothing, but watched as Mrs Peters' hand went towards the bristles that extruded from the girl's cunt. Jess groaned as it was abruptly pulled out, leaving her pussy emptier than ever.

Sardonically observing Lee's aroused state, the manageress asked him, 'Would you like your dick to replace the brush handle for Miss Sanders? I'm sure that right now she is feeling particularly in need of filling, and I know you have a cock worthy of the job.'

Without raising his head, Lee replied, 'Thank you, Mrs Peters, I would.'

'Then assist me.'

Swiftly Jess's bindings were untied. It felt strange to be free, and the clerk's shoulders cracked as she moved, flexing her arms and legs to get her blood circulating again. Jess wasn't allowed her freedom for long however, as Mrs Peters yanked her arms sharply behind her back, re-tying her wrists, and shoving her into the larger and more comfortable teacher's chair, her butt on the very edge of the seat, her legs spread.

'As you are aware, Master Philips, I consider patience one of life's greatest virtues, a lesson I think, by the look of desperation that is shining so blatantly in Miss Sanders' eyes, it is high time she learnt.'

'Yes, Mrs Peters.' Lee deflated slightly as he realised he would have to wait a little longer for his reward, but felt better when Laura passed him the paintbrush, knowing precisely what he was supposed to do with it.

Jess, her eyes wide, her throat drier than ever, watched as Lee ran the brush's soft bristles between his fingers. Kneeling before Jess, he placed the tip of the paintbrush on the very end of her right nipple. Gasping with shock at the sensitivity of the touch, Jess began to shiver against the sweeping strokes Lee focused on her breast.

'I must congratulate you, Master Philips.' Mrs Peters spoke with approval. 'You have an excellent technique there, arousing, and stimulating, without being quite enough to make your subject come.'

Jess groaned. *Why wouldn't they let her come?* As the deliciously torturous brush moved onto her left tit, tears of desire and frustration gathered at the corner of her eyes. She knew she was minutes away from begging. Begging to be fucked, begging to be allowed to come; begging for a warm mouth to come to her pussy, her chest, her mouth.

Her quivers turned to shakes as her stomach knotted with the build up of a fast approaching climax.

A gesture from Laura and Lee dropped the brush, causing tears of desperation to course down Jess's cheeks. 'Now, Miss Sanders, you have to learn to pace yourself. This is as much for our enjoyment as yours, and we are not ready to let you come yet.'

Blinking in disbelief at her superior's words, Jess felt the tears dry against her face, as once again the brush was employed by Lee, this time along her tethered arms, her unsteady legs and her taut stomach. Concentrating hard on not pleading for more direct attention, Jess tried to ignore the growing ache between her legs, and the increasingly obvious presence of Lee's erection.

Jess's persistent moans turned to helpless whimpers as Mrs Peters finally broke the tension. 'You may remove your clothes, Lee.'

The young man moved with uncaring speed and Jess gulped as she saw the neatly circumcised penis that was pointing at her hungrily, slide into the waiting rubber.

Ordered to sit up straight, Jess obeyed as the barman gratefully sank his length into Jess's slick snatch. Their mutual sighs of relief made Mrs Peters issue a sharp sneering laugh. 'So young and so desperate.'

Picking up the brush, the manageress began to stroke the cream bristles back over Jess's tormented nipples, as Lee heaved against her, slapping his backside and balls against her in his urgency to come.

Jess screamed out her climax, her body rocking in shocked pent up pleasure.

As Jess slumped against the barman, Mrs Peters dropped the brush to the floor. 'You see, Miss Sanders, some thing's are so much better if they are promised, but withheld for a while. If you are made to wait, you appreciate things all the more. Don't you think?'

'Yes, Mrs Peters.' Jess spoke automatically through breathless lips. There really wasn't anything else she could say.

Chapter Six

JESS COULDN'T DISGUISE THE wince as she sat down. The bruises she'd received the previous day were blooming across her flesh, and a matching flush of shame covered her face as she saw Lee hasten past her office door.

Switching her computer on, Jess daren't lift her eyes from the screen, not wanting to accept the quiet need she had recognised in Lee's expression. A need she had glimpsed gaping back at her from her reflection in the bathroom mirror that morning.

As Jess blindly stared at an email request for an accommodation booking, she nervously wondered where Mrs Peters was. There was a fascinating darkness surrounding her boss, something dangerous and new, and she feared, addictive. Jess had no doubt that she should get a million miles away from her; from the whole place. Yet here she was, back at her desk, her pulse hammering a little too fast, and her palms clammy, as if she was waiting for something to happen, which if she was honest with herself she was.

Forcing herself to concentrate on the monitor, Jess did her best to close her mind to the events that had dominated her brief period of employment at the Fables. She had almost succeeded in focusing on her work, when a sharp voice made her jump. 'I would like you to place a call for me, Miss Sanders.'

Mrs Peters had an expression of mild amusement on her face as she observed the clerk's red cheeks turn a deeper crimson. A frisson of anticipation ran through the manageress at the thought of what she had in store for the new girl over the coming weeks. Lessons that would ultimately help Miss Sanders fulfil her role as the new assistant on the fifth floor.

'A call?'

'To this gentleman.' Laura passed Sam Wheeler's business card over to Jess, and folded her arms impatiently as the clerk fumbled over the telephone keypad.

Holding the receiver to her ear, Jess waited for the call to be picked up. 'Mr Wheeler?' Jess paused while she listened for the required confirmation. 'I have a Mrs Laura Peters for you, sir, one moment please.'

Jess passed the phone to Mrs Peters, who without pausing to exchange any sort of greeting, spoke into the receiver. 'Lovely picture thank you.' Hanging up before Sam had a chance to say anything at all, she handed the phone back to the clerk. Mrs Peters' face gave nothing away as she left the room, leaving Jess physically shaking in her chair. She'd expected to be told to accompany her employer, to be instructed to observe or take part in some event on the fifth floor. Jess was shocked to realise that not only was she disappointed to have been left behind, but her body had already gone into arousal overdrive.

Taking a draft of water from the bottle on her desk, she took some calming breaths, trying to ignore her slick pussy and tight breasts, telling herself not to be so stupid. Yet, while she had been mentally preparing herself for almost anything, Jess hadn't been prepared for nothing. The tiny element of concentration she'd had evaporated into thin air, as she realised with increasing frustration that she had acted exactly as Mrs Peters had intended.

Lee opened his eyes as commanded and stared directly at the floor below him. His arms and legs ached, but he said nothing. Complaining to Miss Sarah was always a waste of breath.

She stood in the dim candlelight of the dusty dungeon, freshly attired in black patent thigh-length boots, a lace-up black basque, and nothing else. Her long hair hung around her shoulders, and, as she dropped the whip she'd been using to punish Lee's backside, she bent forward to kiss the worst of his bruises.

The Medieval-style wooden rack, against which the barman was tied, was already at half stretch, but Miss Sarah hadn't finished with him yet. Lee bit back a whimper as his arms were pulled another half centimetre forward while, face down, his torso remained captured by a series of thick leather straps across his back.

'You are getting accustomed to this, young man.' Miss Sarah reached a hand through a gap in the framework to stroke his cock, causing Lee to let out an involuntary moan of longing.

In response, Miss Sarah pinched his tip, making him cry out in shock. 'I think you enjoy my rehearsals in the dungeon better than some of my clients enjoy the real thing.' She picked the whip back up, and began to trace the end over his blotched arse.

A click behind her alerted the dominatrix to the opening of the door. She inclined her head in greeting as Mrs Peters entered Room 50. 'I hope you will excuse the intrusion. I wondered how Master Philips was composing himself today.' Laura approached the trussed barman, smoothing a palm across his tacky forehead. 'Very good I see. Better than our new little secretary. She is a nervous wreck, and it seems, can't wait for the next lesson. The silly girl hasn't yet worked out that waiting *is* her next lesson.' Gesturing for Miss Sarah to continue with her pseudo-torture, she said, 'I confess I find her a curious creature, and hope we can get through this period of inactivity fairly quickly.'

Miss Sarah said nothing, but the involuntary raise of an eyebrow gave her surprise at her superior's impatience away.

'I see you are confused by my interest in the young woman.' Laura danced her fingers over Lee, enjoying the increasing quiver of his flesh.

'Yes, madam.' Miss Sarah lowered her eyes a little, sensible of the requirement to appear at least slightly meek in the company of her employer. After all, it had only been six months since she had been the new girl at the whim of Mrs Peters' particular brand of education. Miss Sarah had known she was born to this life however, and hadn't batted an eyelid when Mrs Peters approached her while she worked in Reception.

'You must watch the recordings I have been making of Miss Sanders progress. She is naive and intensely curious, as well as naturally submissive.' Mrs Peters sighed. 'She is, however, still in possession of more of her teenage puppy fat than many of our clients would like. A shame to give in to modern ideas about weight, but the paying customer is always right, I suppose. I am sure I can rely on you to construct a suitable and rewarding exercise programme for her.'

Sarah smiled sardonically. 'It'll be a pleasure,' she said, before she brought her attention back to Lee's arms and turned the cogs that stretched them out one more notch. Despite all his training, Lee began to whimper almost imperceptible words of purposeful frustration. Laura, taking no notice of his discomfort, trailed her fingers through the dark hairs that surrounded his rigid cock. 'Master Philips, I imagine Miss Sarah told you to remain silent.'

On a nod from Mrs Peters, the dungeon mistress brought the whip back down on to Lee's arse, just as her boss wrapped a palm around his solid shaft, squeezing it firmly.

With an immense groan of relief and defeat, Lee's body shuddered to an illegal climax, spunking his load across the wooden floor below him.

Miss Sarah didn't raise her voice; her tone of disapproval was enough to send ripples of delicious fear through Lee's skin. 'That was unfortunate.' She turned to Mrs Peters. 'I must apologise for that pitiful display, madam. After your kind words about his self-control Master Philips has disgraced himself.'

Laura's face remained passive as she regarded her assistant. 'I suggest you release him and make him clean up the mess he's made.'

Miss Sarah, her own colour heightening as she wondered if Mrs Peters blamed her for the boys' failure, took out her uncertainty on Lee. Unstrapping her prisoner, she pointed to the floor. 'You will lick that up.'

Lee swayed as he stood next to the rack. He almost protested, but thinking better of it, crawled under the racks frame, and began to scoop up his spent come with his tongue.

Satisfied that Lee was doing as he was told, Laura turned to Miss Sarah. 'And how are you holding up, Miss Sarah?' Laura slid a hand between her employee's naked thighs. 'Managing to control your own desires adequately I hope?'

Keeping her eyes fixed on Lee, Miss Sarah invisibly swallowed her reactions as the expert fingers manipulated her clit. 'I believe I am keeping my needs in check, Madam.'

'Well done, Miss Sarah,' The manageress, her own well practised detachment in operation, rubbed the juice on her fingertips together, before pushing a digit up inside the dominatrix. 'I can see my training, and your continuing position on the fifth floor, have taught you far more self-discipline than many of your predecessors ever achieved.'

'Thank you, Mrs Peters.' Miss Sarah spoke carefully, aware that her liquid was running freely now, and she had to work hard on not pushing herself down on the frustratingly thin finger that was circling her opening.

'I believe you should be rewarded for your services.' Laura, still speaking as though she felt nothing but professional pride, moved her hand away, and began to undo her colleague's basque, freeing her squashed tits. She looked at them critically. 'Forgive me, I'd forgotten how beautiful they are.'

Turning her attention back to the grovelling barman Laura said, 'That will do, Master Philips.'

Lee sat up on his haunches, semen smeared around his mouth and chin.

'Sit here please.' Laura pointed to a chair she'd had designed especially for the dungeon. Its solid seat was interrupted by the extrusion of an incredibly smooth dildo moulded into the wood, positioned at the perfect angle to be inserted into the anus of the person who sat on it. This, along with a series of attached multi-purpose straps and chains, made it the perfect addition to the room.

Moving carefully, Lee, amazed by what he was being allowed to witness, reached his hands obediently behind him and gingerly pulled open his wounded butt cheeks as, gulping back the initial gut wrenching feeling of invasion, he very slowly sodomised himself.

Once the barman was safely impaled, Mrs Peters caught hold of his arms, and pulled them behind him, securing them to the back of the chair with the chains provided for the purpose. Nodding with satisfaction, and understanding just how badly Lee would want to move, she said, 'You will stay perfectly still.'

'Yes, madam.' Lee spoke through gritted teeth, his need to slide himself up and down against the wooden shaft clearly evident in the fast recovery rate of his cock, which poked hopefully towards the two women.

Miss Sarah's eyes widened, betraying the first faint signs of her own cravings, as her boss took her left nipple between her fingers, and pinched it hard.

'Very good.' Mrs Peters pinched the other one much harder, waiting for a visible reaction. 'Again I'm impressed. But what will happen when I do this?' The manageress bent to her colleague and engulfed her right nipple in her mouth, lightly flicking her tongue over and around the dark brown teat. As she worked, Laura could feel Sarah's body stiffen and her breasts become taut, but still she didn't move or make the slightest sound.

Changing her attention to the other nipple, Mrs Peters turned her licks to bites, grazing her teeth around the nipple, pulling the tip out as far as it would go.

The sound of a heavy grunt that filled the air, but it did not come from Miss Sarah, but from Lee, as he observed the show before him, his backside heavy and unbelievably full, his cock painfully hard and neglected.

Laura stood back and assessed the situation. This had already become a competition, and both women knew it. As Lee watched, he wondered how long it would take before Miss Sarah's iron-clad resolve broke and Mrs Peters managed to reduce her to a begging mass. Or perhaps the younger woman would risk further punishment and win. He wouldn't have liked to be betting on the outcome.

Miss Sarah's feet remained perfectly planted against the dusty floor and her eyes remained lowered, as Laura went to retrieve some implements from a row of rather threatening-looking hooks that ran the length of the dungeon walls. Each held an object of chastisement, torture, and devious pleasure.

Having selected two sharp toothed silver clamps, Mrs Peters steadily sucked Miss Sarah's right nipple to a hot hard point, before snapping a clamp in place. The dungeon mistress bit her lips together, but no sound escaped as her left side received the same treatment, making her tits flush as the blood rushed around her globes in response to the assault. Then, unbuckling the straps that kept the rack horizontal, Mrs Peters pivoted it around, and secured it into its vertical position.

Understanding what was expected of her, Miss Sarah voluntarily stood within the racks confines, allowing her arms and legs to be strapped to its sides so that she was spread-eagled within the device in which she had "entertained" so many paying guests. 'Magnificent.' Mrs Peters kissed her full on the lips, squeezing the already abused breasts between her fingers.

This time Miss Sarah couldn't help but utter a stifled groan of pain and desire, as sweat began to dot across her forehead.

Lee observed the smirk of satisfaction on Mrs Peters face as she collected a paddle from its hook and, moving behind Miss Sarah, began to smack it against her backside, while simultaneously reaching a hand around her waist, and scratching her clit with one fingernail.

The first noticeable quiver came after the fifth strike.

Lee had been counting them, each slap resonating through his own body as he flinched in sympathy against the wooden dildo.

Taking her hand away from Miss Sarah's pussy, Laura slipped her own dress from her shoulders. Totally naked, the manageress knelt and began to lick her tongue over the other woman's nub.

This time the whine that escaped from the dungeon mistress's mouth was clearly audible, and the familiar surge of power that kept Mrs Peters in this job shot down her spine as her companions resolve begin to crack. Poking her tongue faster into the slick pussy juice, she inched her hands up the flawless body, twisting the nipple clamps until Miss Sarah began to pant, and unbidden moisture gathered at the corner of her eyes. Lee could see how her clamped lips were held together and her stomach rose up and down swiftly, as Miss Sarah tried not to be defeated by her body's craving for satisfaction.

As if coming out in sympathy with the dungeon's latest victim, Lee began to pull hopelessly on his bindings, wishing he could wank himself to the climax he so badly needed. Abruptly he stopped. Mrs Peters was staring directly at him. The barman shrank back. He knew he would be punished for that later. His pulse raced even faster, as he wondered how.

Moving back to the tool hooks Mrs Peters quietly considered her next move, before selecting a large double dildo. Her own pussy, if she cared to admit it, was desperate to be filled and she couldn't help but think back to her encounter with Sam Wheeler, and wonder how he would react to her next move in the game. Easily positioning one end of the weapon into her cunt, she remembered how well the artist and fitted inside her, and felt an unfamiliar sensation of longing for that one particular dick, rather than cocks in general. Not allowing that disconcerting thought to linger, she retuned to her dishevelled counterpart, stoking the free end of the dildo over and around Miss Sarah's clit. How badly do you want his inside you?'

Miss Sarah said nothing, but she watched the fake dick like a hawk.

'Very badly I would say, judging by the amount of pussy juice that is being wasted down here.' Laura pressed the phallus tip against the entrance to the shaved mound. 'Perhaps you'd like me to lick you some more. I know you enjoy that, however hard you pretend not to.'

Miss Sarah opened her mouth to speak but no words came out as Mrs Peters hands joined the dildo in circling, but not touching the source of her body's craving.

Lee's mouth, already dry, felt as if it was going to cleave shut as he watched them. The sight of Miss Sarah at the edge of control, of wanting to be fucked as badly as he did, was too much. He knew that if he didn't focus very hard over the next few minutes he was going to come himself, whether someone touched him or not.

'So what do you think, Miss Sarah? Shall I plug you, or shall I just sort myself out?' Laura stepped away from the frame, and fixed her gaze on Sarah's while she eased the dildo's length slowly in and out of herself.

Silence seemed to consume the room for a moment, and then, just as Lee thought she would make it, Miss Sarah spoke, 'Please, madam, fuck me.' Her voice, still remarkably calm, had an undeniable hunger to it and was all the encouragement her boss required as she plunged the doubler into Miss Sarah.

Pulling the clamps from her tits, Mrs Peters feasted on their wounds for a moment as she rode her assistant. Then as her captive started to mewl louder she fastened her mouth to Miss Sarah's and they kissed as savagely as they screwed.

Lee couldn't help it. His spunk shot across the room for the second time that morning as he witnessed the bound mistress succumb to the dominance of her superior with a final cry of release; a release echoed by Mrs Peters' body, but without the undisciplined sound effects.

Freeing Miss Sarah a few minutes later, Mrs Peters said, 'You are indeed an expert in your field, Miss Sarah. Thank you for such a satisfying demonstration of your self-control. No wonder your clients are always so keen to return.'

Gently manoeuvring the strain from her shoulders, Miss Sarah thanked Mrs Peters, and then, as if nothing had happened, turned to Lee. 'You were not given permission to come.'

Lee lowered his eyes, but felt it best not to speak.

'Do you require me to punish him further, Mrs Peters?'

Laura's eyes narrowed. 'I think perhaps he has begun to enjoy his punishments too much. He can clean this lot up and then return to the bar.'

She looked steadily at Lee. 'And you are not to wank for 24 hours. I shall know if you do.'

Chapter Seven

ALTHOUGH SHE HAD VISITED the majority of the facilities provided by the hotel, until now Jess had managed to avoid the gymnasium. The bookings to use the spa and sports equipment were handled by a separate reception at the entrance to the gym, and the closest Jess had got to it was to point the Fables guests in the right direction.

Waiting just inside the sports hall, Jess was reminded of the horror of games lessons at school, the humiliation of the changing rooms, and the hour of hell she'd endured three times a week when she'd totally failed to be good at any sport at all. A humiliation that had stayed with her, putting her off all sport for the rest of her life.

She hated the smell of the place, the sort of antiseptic chlorine-style aroma with an undercurrent of sweat. The air felt heavy and trapped, as if impatient for the day's activity to get underway. Even though it was only seven in the morning, Jess could see two eager tennis players making their way to a court at the far side of the hall, their footsteps echoing against the floor.

Notepad and pen firmly to hand, Jess looked around impatiently for a member of the sports staff to arrive. The gymnasium had been closed for a safety and stock check, and Jess was required to take notes of any adjustments or purchases that needed to be made. She checked her watch again; her accomplice was already ten minutes late. She was just considering reporting back to Reception when she saw Miss Sarah approaching, suitably attired in a figure hugging Lycra sports top and leggings.

For a fleeting second she considered it a possibility that Miss Sarah was coming to help her stock take, but dismissed the idea as ridiculous. She could have been coming for a workout and hadn't been told the gym was closed for the morning. There was no doubt that the woman *did* work out. Jess had seen the physical results of the way the dominatrix kept herself in trim.

I've been set up. The familiar prickle of sweat crept up her spine, as she did her best to shake the thought from her almost continually lust focused mind. Gripping her stationery, and feeling frumpy in her black trousers and white blouse, Jess wondered what was going to happen to her now.

'Miss Sanders.'

'Miss Sarah?' The greeting was not exactly friendly, but at least it stopped short of frosty.

'I have been sent to inform you that the stock take has been postponed until 9 a.m. A far more civilised hour, don't you think?'

Jess didn't reply, her eyes straying to the bunch of keys in Miss Sarah's hand.

'I always workout here. Where do you go?'

'I don't. I can't really afford to join a gym.'

Dismissing this as a minor matter, Miss Sarah replied, 'But can you afford not to? Besides, free use of this gym is available to all Fables staff before eight in the morning, and after nine at night. Did no one tell you?'

'No they didn't, but to be honest I'm not keen on exercise anyway.'

'That ...' the older woman regarded Jess very carefully, '... is all too obvious. I think you should accompany me.' She unlocked the door to the gym and waited for a reluctant Jess to push her way through the double doors.

Four exercise bicycles, some rowing machines, a variety of lifting weights, and numerous other ways to voluntarily exhaust yourself, met Jess's gaze.

She knew she wasn't as fit as she ought to be and that she was more curvy than slim, but if she didn't care about that, and was healthy, then so what?

'I have a confession.' The expression on Miss Sarah's face confirmed Jess's suspicions that this was not an accidental meeting. 'Mrs Peters has asked me to take on a task in addition to my usual duties.'

The paper between Jess's fingers began to feel damp as the foreboding that had been nagging her surged forward. 'What task?'

'Mrs Peters is happy with your progress – on the whole. There are issues that need attention however, improvements that need to be made.' The fifth floor's deputy began to pace around the gym, her fingers running lovingly over the shiny metal machines. 'Our clients have requirements we are duty bound to meet, however clichéd they might be.'

'Please, Miss Sarah, what task?'

'Personally, I think Mrs Peters is wrong. No need to look so shocked. I happen to know this room is not bugged, so I can do and say what I like. I'm also confident that you are not foolish enough to share my thoughts on this.'

Still unsure exactly what Miss Sarah was suggesting, Jess simply agreed that she did indeed know when to keep her mouth shut.

'She thinks your over-round figure is attractive. You are, after all, simply a shorter version of her own shape, but she concedes that the customers tend to prefer slim waists and slender hips along with a large chest.'

Jess swallowed nervously. She could see where this was going, and she didn't like it.

'I, on the other hand, think a strict regime of exercise will not only get rid of that excess fat, it will install in you some much needed discipline and obedience.'

Trying to think when her obedience could possibly have been questioned, Jess's eyes followed Miss Sarah as she continued to stride around the gym, stopping every now and then to caress the equipment.

'And as I'd heard the gym was going to be closed to guests for a while today, I arranged things so that you and I can make a start on the routine I have put together for you.'

'But I don't have time.' Jess knew there was no point in telling her she didn't want to take part, but the pile of work on her desk made what she said perfectly true.

'You do. I have arranged things.'

'But …'

'Enough. You are our employee; consider this one of those "other duties" in your contract. Now, please remove your outer garments; there is no way you can exercise in those.'

Shooting a look of uncertainty towards the doors in case anyone else was about to come in, Jess reluctantly slipped off her shoes and began to undo the buttons of her shirt.

'Don't worry, I've locked the doors.' Miss Sarah went over to a pile of mats in the corner and pulled out three, laying them together on the floor, forming a softer surface on which to work. 'Hurry up, girl, we only have an hour and then you have a stock take to do.'

Peeling her shirt off and tugging down her trousers,

Jess stood in her white satin underwear, her arms crossing self-consciously over her chest.

'For goodness' sake, girl, after six months working here, seeing you semi-naked is hardly going to shock me.'

Acknowledging that for the truth it was, Jess forced herself to lower her arms.

'Right, come here please.' Miss Sarah pointed to the spot directly in front of her on the mats.

Her body shaking, Jess obeyed, her bare feet sticking a little against the plastic surface.

Placing her hands on Jess's elbows, Miss Sarah then levered her arms up so that the clerk was standing with them out at right angles to her body. 'I want you to keep you arms there. You are not to move. While it is important to tone up that stomach and shave some fat off those hips and your arse, it is equally important to increase your upper body strength, but without decreasing that generous chest of yours.'

Without taking her eyes off her student, Miss Sarah reached for a water bottle, and filled it from the cooler before taking a long swig. 'Hydration is very important.'

Jess, her arms already aching from being held stiff at an unaccustomed angle for so long, could almost taste the chilled liquid as it ran down Miss Sarah's throat.

'Two more minutes and I'll let you have some water.'

Sitting down cross-legged on the mat in front of Jess, the other woman looked up at her thoughtfully. 'I bet you're beginning to feel all hot. I might let you take your bra off in a while. It's a shame to keep that chest hidden away. I'll see how well behaved you are – we could call it a reward for doing as you're told.'

It hadn't occurred to Jess that her chest was getting warm; she'd been concentrating so hard on not putting her arms down and relaxing the muscles, which had begun to

75

scream for some relief, she hadn't thought of anything else. Now the idea had been put into her head her breasts felt clammy, and her nipples began to chaff at the inside of her bra cups.

'One more minute.' Miss Sarah looked calm as she sat sipping the cold water, watching the perspiration that was gathered on Jess's forehead.

The clerk couldn't believe how much staying perfectly still was hurting her. The longing for a drink battled with the need to lower her arms as she shuffled her feet a fraction, trying to shift some of the tension that was coursing down her back.

'You moved.' The other woman sounded more resigned than cross. 'Shame, you won't be rewarded with free tits now.'

'I couldn't help it! This hurts so much.'

'Good. Your stamina is pitiful and needs improving. You have 20 seconds left.'

Counting down in her head, her teeth gritted, Jess kept her feet firmly glued to the floor.

'Time up.'

Jess found she couldn't lower her arms as quickly as she'd have liked to. Her muscles had seized, and the only way to manoeuvre them was slowly.

Miss Sarah rose from the floor and passed over the bottle. 'Here, you must keep your fluids up.'

Gratefully, Jess glugged back some water, flexing her feet, legs and shoulders as she did so.

'I'd like you to lie on your back on the mats now, with your arms stretched out above your head and your knees bent.'

Glad to at least be lying down, Jess obliged, surprised by how comfortable it was to have her limbs pulled out in a different direction for a moment.

'Bring your arms down and place them under your head.'

Jess's hair felt hot between her fingers as she listened to the next instruction. 'You will raise both your legs a fraction off the floor, hold them for the count of two, and then lower them. Begin.'

It was harder than it sounded, and Jess was soon struggling to hold her legs in the air for even the count of one. The perspiration that had dotted her forehead turned to sweat, and she could feel droplets run between her cleavage as her breathing became laboured.

'Honestly, Miss Sanders, you're in an even worse state than I feared.' The mistress stood astride Jess's stomach. 'Keep going.' Staring down at Jess's face, she tilted the water bottle slightly, and as Jess watched a tiny drizzle of water began to fall, almost as if in slow motion towards her chest.

The second it hit, Jess cried out, it was so cold it almost burnt her hot flesh, and she stopped moving as the liquid seeped into her bra.

'I told you to keep going.' Miss Sarah held the bottle steady, and the drip drip of water continued to trickle across Jess's cleavage and bra, running down her stomach while she struggled to keep her legs moving. 'Hold in those stomach muscles.'

Openly panting with the effort, Jess's breasts had changed from being hot and uncomfortable to being soaked with a sodden bra clinging to her skin, making her nipples more enlarged than ever.

After three more lifts, Miss Sarah righted the water bottle. 'Stop.'

Jess's legs positively crashed to the floor with exhaustion, not moving as her companion crouched next to her head and whispered, 'That was pathetic – how on earth are you going to manage the sit ups you are about to do?'

Shaking her head from side to side, Jess cried out, 'I can't. I'm sorry, I just can't.' Every muscle in her body was tight and sore from the unaccustomed workout she hadn't even been allowed to warm up for.

'But you can, and you will.' Miss Sarah sat astride Jess's legs, trapping her in place against the gym mats. Splayed fingers ran provocatively around the outline of Jess's tits, igniting every nerve in her body. 'I have an incentive scheme in mind. Sit up.'

Jess struggled to her elbows and Miss Sarah deftly reached around her back and undid her bra, peeling it off with a sticky sucking sound. Then shuffling forward, she licked the nipple of each breast just once, sending shock waves of pleasure through Jess's tired frame.

'Each time you sit up properly, you will have a nipple tongued.'

Wishing this wasn't such a strong incentive, but privately knowing it was Jess nodded, her face flushed with shame.

'Good girl, I knew you would.'

With a deep breath, her hands behind her head, Jess sat up, but failed to get as far as Miss Sarah and sank back in defeat.

'Again.'

Jess winced as she rose upwards, determined to reach the mouth that was already parting to take in her right teat. The contact was fleeting and moist and delicious, and Jess suddenly found she had the hidden reserves to move again, this time being rewarded on the left side. Five sit ups later and Miss Sarah began to laugh, before saying, 'Enough,' and Jess sagged back, relieved, but instantly missing the stimulation and violently aware of the heat that was coursing between her legs.

Rising abruptly, Miss Sarah returned to her usual business-like demeanour. 'Up.'

Taking her time to rise to her quaking legs Jess did as she was told, before drinking from the water bottle that was offered to her.

'A quick cycle I think.' Jess walked unsteadily to the nearest bike and went to sit down, but was stopped. 'These need to be put in place first.'

Jess's eyes goggled at the tiny set of love balls Miss Sarah had produced from nowhere. Tug those pants down, girl and open those legs.'

Clumsily, the clerk did as she was told, almost coming as the slender fingers slipped the weighted spheres easily inside her wet channel, before pulling up the knickers to keep them in place.

'Cycle.'

With every laboured turn of the pedals the love balls slid around inside her, and Jess could feel the knot of an orgasm rise in her like fire.

'Hold in those stomach muscles. Keep control, girl! Consider this a practice for when I make you do this exercise without knickers on!'

Jess pulled in her tummy for all she was worth; the tighter she clenched her muscles the more the balls stayed still. But each time she lost concentration, the heavy spheres rolled towards the mouth of her vagina, and Jess had to re-double her efforts to keep them contained; their pressure adding to the need she felt magnifying by the second. By the time Miss Sarah shouted 'Stop', tension oozed from every pore of Jess's shattered body.

The moment she stopped pedalling the love balls swung within her, and unable to stop it, a climax zipped through her untutored flesh and she shook and shuddered against the bike. Not daring to look at Miss Sarah, Jess quickened herself, the disapproving silence of the room enveloping her.

Her voice surprisingly neutral, the dominatrix said, 'Come here, and pass the balls to me.' Tugging her knickers down a little, the balls plopped out of their own accord. Jess shamefacedly gave them back to Miss Sarah. *Why isn't she cross?*

'We are almost out of time. I'm sure I don't need to tell you these sessions are to become a regular thing, and, if you do as you're told, then I will be rewarding you – occasionally. Now, we'll finish with a run. This is only a small room, so I suggest four circuits of the perimeter.'

Jess looked at her in exhausted horror. 'I can't.'

'Not like that you can't, certainly. Take those knickers off; you need to get some air down there, girl.'

No longer caring about anything but the possibility of a rest, Jess dragged the wet satin away, and following the direction that Miss Sarah was pointing in, began to jog around the room. Her breasts swayed madly and the air seemed to caress her body, inflaming it all over again.

Observing the figure that was obeying her, knowing she'd only have to say the word and she'd willingly allow herself to be fucked, Miss Sarah frowned to herself. Mrs Peters might have designs on forming this girl into the ideal submissive assistant, but she began to wonder if this girl could be dangerous. She had spent a long time building up her guest list; did Miss Sarah really want Miss Sanders muscling in on that?

Chapter Eight

SAM COULDN'T CONCENTRATE. HE looked again at the plan he was roughing out, or was supposed to be roughing out. Two glaring mistakes jumped out at him. Mistakes he would never normally make. 'Bloody woman.' Sam grabbed an eraser and attacked the paper.

The image of Laura Peters, however, was proving harder to rub out. Every time he closed his eyes, every time he opened them, with every stroke of the pencil he saw her, felt her flesh, saw the never ending quest for intimate satisfaction shining in her bewitching eyes.

In an attempt to clear his mind of the graphic pictures their porn-style sex had implanted in his head, Sam forced himself think of all the men she must have known, and probably all the women as well. No. He stopped thinking about the women. That would tip his erotic musings over the edge completely.

Moving from his desk, Sam flung down his pencil and went to the window, failing to see the view outside. He should never have left the picture and business card. It was an open invitation for her to get in touch, to ask him over to the hotel for a drink or something, and yet all she'd done was curtly say, thank you, before hanging up on him. 'What did you expect?' Sam muttered angrily to himself. 'You were just a shag for her, just someone she wanted to fuck, rather than someone she was paid to fuck.'

He smiled ruefully, aware of the irony of the situation, remembering all the women in his past, all the ones he'd slept with and left. He'd used them. 'Well now I know how that feels then.'

Pouring himself an extra strong cup of coffee, Sam stopped staring blankly into the distance and returned to his desk. Adjusting the angle-poise lamp, he began to draw in the floor levels of the building proposal, before transferring the whole draft onto his computer.

'I'll give you one more day, Laura Peters, and then I'm coming to find you, whether you like it or not.'

It had been a very quiet 48 hours at Fables. Business was not exactly dead, but by no means was it as hectic as usual.

'It's 'cause we're between conferences,' Lee told Jess, as they both sat, not really knowing what to say beyond small talk, in the staffroom for their lunch break. 'We never get much activity on the in between days, just the usual overnight business men and well, the fifth floor customers – you know.'

Jess stared down at her lap as Lee finished speaking. Silence began to stretch between them, becoming an almost tangible presence as they sat on opposite sides of a rickety wipe down table. Jess fiddled with her coffee mug, trying not to remember how good Lee's hands had felt on her skin, or how fantastic his cock had felt when it slid between her legs. She hardly dared to look at the barman in case her expression gave her thoughts away, but there was something she simply had to ask him, and who knew when they'd have another opportunity to be alone.

'Why do you stay here?' Conscious that her voice had

come out rather huskier than usual, Jess twirled her coffee cup in small circular movements on the table, glancing up at Lee through her fringe.

'The same reason you do.'

It wasn't the answer she'd expected. 'What do you mean?'

Lee sighed, and drank down the dregs from his tea. 'To see what will happen next. To see if I can handle it, to discover my limits.'

'Oh.' Jess thought back to the second exercise session she'd had that morning, and the feel of Miss Sarah's teeth as they'd bitten rather than licked her nipples as she'd done her sit ups. Was that why she was still working there, to see how far she could be pushed?

As if reading her mind Lee said, 'If it wasn't the same for you, you'd have left by now, like those before you.'

Jess stared directly at him now. 'Have there been many?'

'A few.' Lee spoke dismissively, as if the comings and goings of other staff members didn't interest him. 'Some stay for a day, some a week. Some find out how we use the top floor and leave before they've even set eyes on it.'

'How come this place hasn't been closed down then, if so many people know about its private side?'

Lee laughed sharply. 'Honestly, woman, haven't you seen the clients that come and go?'

Surprised by his tone, Jess shook her head. 'No, I just answer the phone and do the emails, remember. Who are they then?'

'They mostly use false names, but that's not important. What is important is that they're usually policemen and women, judges, MPs. Important and wealthy business men and women, the general cliché clients you'd expect. No one else could afford the fifth floor room prices.

We're talking influential people who have no interest in this place closing, and so it doesn't close. All rumours are quashed from the top down.'

'Have you met some of them then?'

'In the course of assisting on the fifth floor you mean?'

'I suppose so, yes.' Jess felt her face glow cherry.

'I have, and so will you.'

'Can I ask you something else?' Lee didn't reply, so Jess continued. 'What's in the final room on the fifth floor?'

Lee stood up, acting as though Jess hadn't asked him anything at all. 'We should get back.'

Jess followed him to the sink, trying to pretend she hadn't noticed the erection that had begun to push out beneath his suit trousers. She felt a strange shimmer of triumph that it may have been caused by him recalling their enforced coupling in the school room a week ago.

Standing behind the barman, waiting while he rinsed out his cup, Jess had an uncharacteristic urge to put her hands on his small neat backside. *No, I don't want to touch it. I want to hit it, hard.* Images of Miss Sarah chastising Master Philips on her first trip to the fifth floor crowded her head, jostling for a place with pictures of Lee brushing her skin in the school room. Jess took a hasty step backwards, shocked by her instincts and mindful that any such move might well be observed as she suddenly wondered if the room had hidden cameras within its walls.

Drying his hands, Lee, turned to face Jess. 'You must have friends and family who've been asking about your new job, what have you told them?'

'My parents live abroad, and most of my friends went to uni and moved away to get jobs and stuff. They just know I have a new admin job in a hotel. I have no intention of telling them more than that.'

'Very wise.' Lee's eyes became shrewder. 'And do you have a boyfriend, girlfriend?'

Jess found herself blushing again, and inwardly cursed herself for doing so. 'No. No one. Not for some time.'

Lee dropped the cloth and seemed to consider before he spoke again. Then, dipping the volume of his voice said, 'You will be careful, won't you.'

'Careful?'

'I suspect Mrs Peters has plans for you. You obviously intrigue her. Be wary, OK?'

'Intrigue her?'

Lee suddenly appeared uncomfortable. 'She hasn't told you about her plans?'

'No.'

'Then perhaps you're not supposed to know.'

'But …' Jess struggled to comprehend how she could intrigue anyone.

Lee glanced around the room furtively, and Jess understood at once that he wasn't sure if the room was bugged or not either. 'I have work to do. Excuse me.'

Jess nodded, aware once again that her pulse rate had been thunderously high and her crotch was wet, yet she was a little mollified by her conviction that Lee was in a similarly lustful state. Washing out her mug, she walked quickly and thoughtfully back to her office.

Laura Peters swung back in her chair and smiled thoughtfully. The girl seemed to have developed a modicum of self-restraint already. She wasn't sure if she was pleased or disappointed that engineering Lee and Jess's break-time to clash hadn't produced the illicit rule breaking and impromptu sex she'd assumed it would.

For a moment she wondered about Lee's reticence

when talking to the new clerk. The boy obviously had more sense than she'd credited him with.

There was a knock at the door and Miss Sarah came in. 'Did they go for it?'

'No.'

Miss Sarah failed to conceal her surprise. 'So my discipline will not be required then?'

'It would seem not. A shame, I was quite looking forward to it.'

The dominatrix's eyes narrowed, once again wondering about Mrs Peters' preoccupation with Miss Sanders.

As if she understood her assistant, Mrs Peters said, 'You think I'm getting hung up on this girl?'

'Well, I ...'

Laura stood up, flicking off the screen of her PC so the image of the now empty staff room disappeared. 'You are an excellent mistress, Miss Sarah, but for a while now I've been searching for someone to fulfil the opposite end of the sexual spectrum. I think perhaps I have found the perfect submissive. You must forgive my seeming obsession. I am merely anxious to see if my inclinations are correct. Many of our clients would be more than a little pleased if I am.'

Miss Sarah inclined her head. 'I can see that would make sense.'

'Well then,' Laura threw her jacket over her shoulders. 'I have a new guest in ten minutes. I look forward to seeing how Miss Sanders and you work together. I would like you to include her in your next session.'

Sweeping regally out of the room Mrs Peters left Miss Sarah seething quietly, while contemplating just how she could include Jess in her next client's routine, and, more importantly, wondering why should she change things just for her. Playing with the girl for fun while she exercised was one thing, but she'd spent weeks building up a trusted relationship with her guests. She'd be damned if she'd risk ruining her reputation just for Miss Jess Sanders.

The call came through only a few moments after Jess had returned to her desk. The tops of her legs felt sticky, and her knickers had been so damp since her body had gone into private overload in the staffroom, that she had disposed of them on a speedy trip to the Ladies, hoping like hell no one was watching. She was to go to Room 53.

When Jess arrived there was a canvas bag hanging on the door handle, with a large note attached. *Miss Sanders, please change before entering.*

Jess had no idea where she was supposed to change, but she didn't dare disobey, so slipping off her shoes, she glanced into the bag. There was hardly anything there. The outfit was so tiny she might as well have been naked, but at least it revealed to her the nature of Room 53.

With shaking hands Jess peeled off the rest of her clothes, leaving only her stockings and suspenders on, cursing that she'd removed her knickers. Dressing with haste in case anybody should pass by, Jess found herself wearing the skimpiest nurse's uniform she'd ever seen. She felt like a cross between a porn star and an advert for a sex-shop. She also, to her surprise, felt almost as sexy as she did nervous.

Low cut over her ample cleavage, and high cut to just above her thigh, Jess knew that if she was asked to bend down for anything her arse would be on view to the whole world. She wriggled within the white material, which was as shiny as PVC and as soft as leather. Jess had no idea what fabric it was, but it felt incredibly sensual against her bare skin.

Standing in her stockinged feet, Jess was about to stuff her own clothes into the canvas bag, when she spotted the nurse's hat tucked in the bottom. Fishing it out she put it over her red bob, feeling more self-conscious by the second.

With her hand on the doorknob Jess hesitated, her heart hammering. Lee's words echoed in her ears, telling her to be careful, telling her they'd push her to her limits. For the hundredth time that day, Jess wondered what Mrs Peters considered to be so special about her? And for the thousandth time, she questioned why she hadn't run away.

Her musings were cut short by the opening of the door from the inside.

'Come on, girl, we have a visitor due.'

Jess was startled to see Miss Sarah and not Mrs Peters standing in the doorway.

'Come on! This room has been paid for. Our guest will be here any minute.' Miss Sarah, looking none too happy and balancing on the highest heels Jess had ever seen, walked purposefully across the room.

Jess trailed dutifully in the mistress's wake, focusing all her attention on the slim swaying body, clad in an outfit as skimpy as her own, but in a pale green that flattered her hair and eyes perfectly.

'Have you been in this room before?' Sarah turned and examined Jess critically, before reaching out and giving her uniform a sharp tug downwards so that even more of her cleavage was revealed. 'That's better. You have an excellent pair of tits, be proud of them.'

Jess was about to say this was new territory for her, when Sarah carried on, 'We need to get your hair sorted though.' She pulled off Jess's hat and tussled her fingers through her bob, somehow making it both tidy and "from the bed sexy" at the same time.

As Miss Sarah busied herself adjusting her own hair, Jess ran her gaze around the room. Despite the fact it was the same size and shape as all the other hotel rooms, there was no mistaking that this was supposed to be a medical examination room. The air felt sterile, the walls were stark white, and every surface shone as if regularly disinfected.

Around two of the walls ran a row of white cupboards, topped with a stainless steel worktop, above which were further cupboards. Along the third wall was a free standing full-length mirror, a height chart, a weighing scales and an IV stand complete with a saline bag. Gaps on the walls were filled with the obligatory art prints that all hospitals and doctor's surgery's hang up to supposedly relax their patients. The final wall simply held the door and a series of coat hooks. Calming classical music wafted from an overhead speaker.

It was the medical examination couch in the very centre of the room that commanded most of Jess's attention however. A cross between a dentist's chair, a gynaecologist's couch and a hospital bed, it was fully automated and could be rendered flat, moved into an upright position, or adopt any position in between. Made of black wipeable plastic, Miss Sarah had covered it with a layer of blue disposable paper.

Satisfied with her appearance at last Miss Sarah turned to Jess. 'This is your first time assisting with a client I believe.'

'Yes, I …' Jess was about to say she hadn't agreed to do this, but Miss Sarah cut sharply through her protests before they began.

'Mrs Peters believes it would do you good to witness me at work. I may occasionally need assistance; it will depend on the will of the client. *Everything* …' she paused to emphasise the point, '… depends on the will of the client. Yes?'

'Of course.' Jess remembered Lee's warning about how important these clients were and a flash of relief that she would probably only watch surged through her, only to find itself mingling with a confused disappointment that she might not be going to take part in the proceedings.

'You will speak only when spoken to. You will do whatever our guest asks you to, *if* they ask. If I wish for your help I will ask our guest for permission first.'

Jess nodded.

'I suggest you stand over there. You will not move unless I request you to do otherwise.' Miss Sarah pointed to the gap between the mirror and the wall mounted height chart, a spot that would ensure she could see everything that happened on the couch, and be seen by the guest that occupied said couch at all times.

There was a knock at the door, and Jess felt her insides freeze. Miss Sarah, as calm as ever, gave Jess a final assessing look and went to answer it.

Just as Miss Sarah's hand reached the handle, she said, 'Don't be alarmed by what I do to this person. It is precisely what they have come here for, and I have been trained to do it.'

As the familiar sensation of being torn between wanting to run and wanting to stay consumed her, sick with foreboding, Jess suddenly knew what it felt like to be a rabbit caught in headlights. Fascinated by the coming brightness, knowing it brought danger, but simply unable to resist …

Chapter Nine

THE GUEST WAS NOT what Jess has been expecting. For a start it was a woman.

Tall, slender, but rather severe-looking in her designer suit and power heels, she put her briefcase down as casually as if she was popping into the doctor's surgery for a general check-up. Neatly cropped black hair was pulled back into a short businesslike pony-tail, and her subtly made-up coal grey eyes swept the room; they lingered rather longer than was comfortable on Jess.

Miss Sarah took the jacket from her client's shoulders. 'Which scenario today, madam?'

'Session B I think.' The woman gave Miss Sarah a half smile, a smile that died as her gaze turned to Jess. 'Is the girl staying?'

Miss Sarah answered the question as bluntly as it had been asked, 'I am training her. Naturally, if you wish her to leave, then I will dismiss her at once.'

There was a brief silence. As Jess's heart thumped inside her ribcage, she wasn't sure if she was hoping to be asked to leave or not.

'She might be a pleasant distraction when things get, shall we say, cramped. She can stay.'

'Very good, madam,' Miss Sarah moved to Jess. 'You may stay, Miss Sanders, but you will not move, and you will not touch yourself.'

Jess exhaled gently as she privately came to terms with the fact that she'd have been disappointed if she hadn't been allowed to witness whatever was about to happen. She already wanted to find out what the woman meant by "cramped".

With a lack of self-consciousness which Jess could only envy, the woman Miss Sarah referred to as madam, striped off her blouse and skirt. standing only in a crimson bra and matching thong, she then allowed Miss Sarah to assist her in the removal of her underwear.

Already finding it difficult to keep in her position against the wall, Jess couldn't prevent her eyes from straying between madam's small breasts and towards her totally shaved pussy.

Her body's reaction to the women in this hotel had been Jess's biggest shock since she'd begun to work at Fables. She'd excused her unexpected arousal by telling herself that Mrs Peters and Miss Sarah were professionals; they exuded a sexiness that was impossible to ignore. This woman, however, was an outsider. Jess was disconcerted to find she was equally turned on by her presence and realised her previous excuses held no water.

The clerk thought back to the evening before, alone at her kitchen table, the local paper open at the page of job advertisements, knowing she should be hunting for alternative employment. Totally convinced she shouldn't even bother getting up and going to Fables in the morning, Jess was equally convinced she would go anyway, that searching for new employment was merely a gesture to her troubled conscience.

Staring at Miss Sarah as she helped the naked woman onto the medical bed, Lee's words echoed in Jess's brain yet again. Did she really want to know how far she could go? Could it be that, by accident, she had stumbled across a side of her sexuality that she actually needed to be fulfilled? Jess shut her eyes, trying to clear the voice from her head that was telling her to accept this as a fact, a voice that seemed all the more shocking because it was her own.

When she finally opened her eyes, Jess found herself looking directly at Miss Sarah. 'Sorry.' A blush covered the clerk's face in the presence of Miss Sarah's displeasure.

'I think Mrs Peters would require you to pay more attention than that, Miss Sanders.'

Rather than risking an audible reply, Jess inclined her head meekly, in the manner she'd seen Lee adopt. Enough to show respect, but not enough to miss what was happening.

Satisfied that Jess was now paying attention, Miss Sarah returned to the client, who was lying perfectly flat on the bed. Raising the woman's head, Miss Sarah undid the ponytail, and placed a cushion beneath her head. Black hair hung loose around the pillow, making madam appear younger and more vulnerable somehow. Then, operating a previously unseen catch from under the bed, Miss Sarah pulled out a wide PVC strap and passed it over madam's stomach, fastening it beneath the opposite side of the bed. Jess could see that it was pulled very tight, for the white band was digging into the flat suntanned stomach, as taut as an elastic band ready to snap.

Madam didn't make a sound as Miss Sarah took both her wrists and levered them high above her head, so they were stretched out beyond the support of the couch. Tying the wrists deftly together with surgical tape, Miss Sarah left them hanging unsupported, before focusing on her customer's ankles.

Jess held her breath as Miss Sarah pushed her guest's

legs up and outwards at the knee, so that they were almost off the bed. Then, with more surgical tape, she began to attach each ankle to madam's thighs, trussing her up so that her channel was at its most visible and exposed.

The clerk could only imagine how uncomfortable the woman must be, yet it was clear from the pertness of her dark brown nipples, and the light sheen glistening around her vagina, that she was excited by her lack of control.

Silently checking each of the bindings she had put in place, Miss Sarah said, 'I am ready. Remember, madam, to stop this session early you must say "Quit", no other word will end this. Yes?'

'Yes.' She confirmed her readiness to begin the game, but madam's tone, and the increased rise and fall of her tethered ribcage told Jess just how keyed up she was.

'Very well.' Miss Sarah adjusted the sound system, and flooded Room 53 with the soothing strains of Beethoven. Then she opened one of the white cupboard doors and brought out a metal tray of medical instruments.

The moment she saw them Jess's stomach contracted. Surely madam didn't get off on that, did she?

A speculum, medical gloves, and a tube of lube lay on the tray. Immediately Miss Sarah snapped on the gloves, but rather than picking up the metal tool that Jess associated with the uncomfortable yet essential smear, Miss Sarah began to stroke a single latex-covered finger over and around madam's nub.

The sound that came from the businesswoman's lips was deep and full of relief.

Jess shot her gaze from Miss Sarah's busy digit, to madam's face and back again. The grey eyes were closed and her thin red lips were clamped together. A sticky trickle of sweat ran down between Jess's shoulder blades as she observed the scene. Her outfit was becoming warmer by the minute, and she could feel her tits chaffing against the inside of the costume. Shuffling her feet, careful not to alert the others to her fidgeting, a gush of liquid oozed from her pussy as she watched madam begin to react more obviously to Miss Sarah's ministrations.

Unable to move her hips or stomach properly, madam's buttocks rose marginally, and her arms swayed a little behind her head. A protracted groan escaped from the client as Miss Sarah added a second finger to the first. Moments later the groan developed into a low whimper, as madam struggled not to beg Miss Sarah to put something inside her soaking pussy.

Suddenly Miss Sarah stood back, causing madam to gulp with loss. 'I believe,' the mistress said slowly, 'that Session B doesn't allow you to make more than "reasonable noise". If you make a row like that again, I shall have to gag you.'

Rather than protest, madam nodded like a chastised child.

Standing to one side of her guest, Miss Sarah placed one gloved hand back over her clit, and the other on the very tip of her right breast. Jess's own nipples grew in aching sympathy as the skilled fingers of the pseudo-nurse played over the nipple, neither holding it nor squeezing it, but merely caressing its tip in a fashion designed to drive the recipient to distraction.

Madam's intense expression of concentration doubled, and Jess could see that her teeth were being ground together in an attempt not to call out.

As Miss Sarah continued to work, the client's body began to shake, making little sucking sounds against the strap. The blue paper that covered the bed had stuck to her back, and tiny dots like tears had gathered at the corners of her shut eyes.

Jess, her own fight against arousal having been given up almost straight away, wondered if she could have withstood such treatment without climaxing already, or without at least begging for permission to come. She suspected not. Not brave enough to turn from the action in case Miss Sarah noticed, Jess tried to decelerate her rapid breathing by thinking about something else, but it was impossible. She was just contemplating what would happen if the client did beg for some attention, when a weak voice from the bed said, 'Please ...'

Miss Sarah instantly ceased her attentions. 'Please?' Her voice was stern. 'To end this, you say "Quit", otherwise you are not supposed to speak.'

'The next stage. Pleaseeeee ... I ...'

Jess studied each woman's reactions carefully. Would Miss Sarah oblige? After all, madam was paying for this.

'A few minutes I think. Then, perhaps I will continue to the next stage. *If* you are good and quiet.'

The tears that had gathered at the corners of madams eyes began to run more freely as Miss Sarah returned to her torturous rubbing. The nipple that hadn't been touched was stiff and hard with neglect, but the one that had been receiving all the attention was bright red, and as Jess watched, she was sure she could see the skin was beginning to crack. Yet it was how madam hadn't climaxed beneath the glove at her crotch that fascinated Jess. The woman's torso was rising up and down, her breathing was laboured and her hands were clasped together above her head. Jess couldn't help speculating how heavy her arms felt as they hung off the bed. She glanced at the clock on the wall, another minute had gone by and the perspiration on madam's forehead had spread to her neck.

Jess bought her palms to her own chest. She couldn't help it. The fabric itself actually felt hot, and her nipples were trying to break out on their own as her tits swelled under the uniform. Cupping her breasts Jess failed to contain the sigh of relief her body gave at the brief moment of physical contact.

Miss Sarah regarded her sharply, her face darkening, but she said nothing as Jess guiltily dropped her arms back to her sides.

Three more strokes of the sore nipple and the dominatrix nurse stepped away from the bed. Once again the abrupt cessation of stimulation made madam cry out. Saying nothing, Miss Sarah picked up the tube of lubricant and squeezed a generous amount between her fingers. She was about to administer it to madam's mound when she stopped. 'I realise this is a deviation from your scenario, but I will allow Miss Sanders to distract you if you wish. I am ashamed to say it appears she cannot be trusted to just stand and observe as I had hoped, so she may as well be of some use to us.'

Madam, her skin flushed with red blotches, had no saliva left in her mouth with which to speak, but inclined her head a fraction, her eyes shining with a lustful desire that belied her exhausted state.

'Miss Sanders come here please.' Jess didn't hesitate. 'I am about to add the speculum to madam. This can be a little uncomfortable; I'd like you to take her mind off things by suckling the neglected teat.'

Jess, her own body shaking, moved to the opposite side of the table, and examined the pert globe that seemed to stare back at her beseechingly. She felt a moment of panic as the two women waited for her to act, Miss Sarah with impatience, madam with a quiet desperation. Knowing she couldn't wait any longer Jess leant forward and engulfed the nipple between her lips. Some previously hidden instinct took over, and she was surprised to discover she knew exactly what to do. Swirling the pleasantly rough tip round her mouth, a frisson of satisfaction flooded her as she heard madam moan with delight. Building in confidence Jess brought a hand to the breast and began to stroke the underside gently in a way she knew she would enjoy herself, while her tongue and lips glided over the soft flesh.

Madam's body stiffened and Jess knew the lube must be being applied. She could imagine all too well how it would feel to have the freezing gel pushed up inside her hot snatch, perhaps with one finger, maybe with two or even three. Jess's pulse tweaked up a notch and she closed her eyes, taking her own craving out on the flesh between her teeth, biting and pinching it, making madam squeak with pain and shake with longing.

The clatter of metal against metal told Jess that Miss Sarah must have picked up the speculum. Then an impulsive jerk from the bed forced Jess to open her eyes again. She saw Miss Sarah below her, easing the fearsome medical instrument in place. To try and divert madam's attention Jess began to slow her licks, making them strong and steady, amazed as the teat hardened even further between her teeth as she grazed the tip.

'Miss Sanders.' Jess stood up at the sound of Miss Sarah's voice. 'Here please.'

Jess couldn't contain her sharp intake of breath when she saw madam's vagina stretched so wide open, clamped in place by the gadget still in Miss Sarah's hand.

'Madam likes to get off on lack of control,' Miss Sarah said in a hushed whisper. 'The sensation of being completely empty and open, when all her body really wants is to be very, very full. That's what does it for her.'

Jess's forehead creased in confusion. 'I see you don't understand, but you will in time.'

Then, with a swift push of the speculum deeper into her client, making her squeal as it reached its capacity, Miss Sarah dropped to her knees. 'I do not want to damage madam internally in anyway, so I will be gauging her movements carefully.'

Jess said nothing, but stared, aghast, at what she was seeing.

The tense silence, punctuated only by madam's stilted breathing, was abruptly broken. 'Make the girl strip.' The words were stilted and slow between pants of air, but there was no denying what madam had asked for.

Miss Sarah hesitated for just a second, unsure whether to punish her client for talking or to grant her request, just to see how Jess would cope. 'You heard madam. Strip before her.'

Despite her desperation to take off the uniform that was suctioned to her flesh, Jess felt another wave of self-consciousness wash over her. It was only the harsh look in Miss Sarah's eyes that spurred her on to do as she was told. Standing next to the head of the bed, madam's watering yet piercing eyes watched as Jess struggled to unstick the fabric that had almost glued itself to her skin. Eventually, without either dignity or finesse, Jess eased the nurse's uniform to the floor, and stood before the businesswoman, very much aware of how dishevelled and damp she must appear.

'I want to feel her tits.'

Miss Sarah nodded, and gestured to Jess to stand behind madam's head, and physically put her breasts into her tethered palms.

The second her chest felt madams grasp clumsily manoeuvre over her sticky flesh, Jess felt her own control slipping. Not knowing what to do with her hands, and convinced she would not be allowed to touch herself where she needed attention most, Jess began to stroke the sweat-soaked hair from madam's eyes. Surely she would say 'Quit' soon; surely she couldn't take much more of this without coming?

Looking over her head, Jess saw Miss Sarah keeping the speculum steady and open, while the air danced around inside madam's opening. Then bending forward, the mistress began to lap her tongue over the client's distended clit.

The mild quaking that had come from madam's body was immediately swapped for a violent shaking, and the speculum was hastily withdrawn, as Miss Sarah continued with her laps. Jess yelped as madam squeezed her tits roughly in response to her overwhelming orgasm.

As she came, madam let go of Jess, and her arms hung limp. It was as if every ounce of her energy had been spent, and all she could do was lie there, her legs still taped together, while her breathing slowly calmed.

Freeing one taped up leg at a time, Miss Sarah massaged the cramped muscles firmly to aid circulation as she eased them flat onto the bed. Instructing Jess to free the wrists, the clerk copied Miss Sarah's actions, and manipulated their clients newly freed limbs with great care, until she was comfortably reclining, floppy but relaxed, on the couch.

'We will leave you to recover yourself, madam. You are free to remain as long as required. Lee will bring you a drink very soon.'

'Thank you, Miss Sarah.' The businesswoman's voice was hoarse, but her austere controlled manner was already beginning to return.

'Come, Miss Sanders.' Miss Sarah led the way to the

100

door.

'One moment,' madam called. 'The girl; I will have her here next time please.'

'Certainly, madam.'

The door to Room 53 had hardly shut behind them when Miss Sarah rounded on Jess. 'How dare you start pleasuring yourself in the presence of a guest.'

'But I couldn't help it, I was so …'

'So what? Don't you think I feel the same? The trick is that you never *ever* show it unless that is what you are required to do at the time?'

'I …'

'You were lucky this time; madam liked you, and miraculously wants you there next time. If it had been someone else you would now be punished.'

Jess didn't know what to say in the face of Miss Sarah's expected anger. Surely it wasn't her fault that she was so stimulated. This was so new to her, after all. She hadn't even asked for this. She was only the clerk!

Miss Sarah's anger dipped into thoughtful silent seething. 'What makes you so bloody special anyway? Why is Mrs Peters so interested in you? And now madam as well!'

Confused, Jess said, 'Special, what do you mean?'

Miss Sarah's words were almost spat out. 'Well it's about time I found out I think … Helping you exercise is one thing, but now the time has come … Follow me.'

Chapter Ten

JESS STUMBLED AS SHE was pushed around a hidden corner at the very end of the corridor and through one of the two doors she'd not noticed before. Putting out a hand to steady herself against the wall, she ducked as the canvas bag containing her clothes flew past her head.

The door slammed shut behind them and Miss Sarah wordlessly strode through her private quarters until she reached the bathroom.

Unsure whether to follow or re-dress, Jess stood for a moment, nervously taking in her surroundings. It was more than a simple hotel room and she realised that Miss Sarah must live at Fables just as Mrs Peters did.

The sound of the shower blasting into life cut through Jess's musings. Feeling cold, and more than a little uncomfortable, she decided to risk Miss Sarah's anger and get dressed while she could.

Fumbling her clothes from the bag Jess found her hands unexpectedly shaky, as if everything that had happened to her and all that she'd witnessed over the past few days had hit her all at once. Hunting for her knickers, and then remembering that she hadn't had them on, Jess couldn't help but wonder what it was that Mrs Peters regarded as special about her, not to mention why it was suddenly making Miss Sarah jealous.

'You had better not be dressing in there.' Miss Sarah's

words were semi-drowned out by the pounding of the water, but the tone of her voice was unmistakable. 'Come here.'

Jess dropped her clothes back to the floor and, aware of the penalties of disobeying, followed the sound of her mistress's voice.

She was not in the shower, but waiting beside it, wasted water cascading into the empty tray. 'Get in.'

Clammy after the sweltering suction of the nurse's uniform, Jess did as she was told. The water was unbelievably hot, but as her flesh adjusted to its temperature and pressure Jess's knotted muscles started to unwind.

'Wash your hair.' Miss Sarah passed Jess a bottle of shampoo. Standing back, her own uniform still in place, she watched every move the clerk made.

Wordlessly Jess circulated a handful of shampoo through her hair, the knots untangling beneath her fingers. When the soap was all washed away, Jess went to step out of the shower, but Miss Sarah signalled for her to stay exactly where she was.

Taking the still steaming shower attachment from its hook, Miss Sarah lowered the head towards Jess, focusing its fast flow onto her left breast. Automatically Jess's hand went up to protect herself from the sharp sting of water, but Miss Sarah knocked it away.

'Put your hands behind your back.'

Jess tried to comply, but the moment her hands came away, her nipple puckered in unexpected discomfort, and her palms came back to her chest.

'So much for you being the ultimate submissive!' Jess couldn't decide if Miss Sarah was pleased or disappointed. 'You can't even stand still in a shower, and I'd thought that by now our exercise training would have installed some discipline and stamina in you. Seems I was wrong.'

Biting back a cry of distress, wondering what Miss Sarah had meant by her "ultimate submissive" comment. Jess forced herself to put her hands behind her back, an action which pushed her breasts further up and out, making them a clearer target for Miss Sarah's water torture.

Keeping the shower head at an even distance from the clerk's body, Miss Sarah switched the high-pressure jet to Jess's right side, making her wince as the agreeable heat quickly changed, becoming first a sore, and then a smarting hurt.

Jess grasped her hands behind her back, her fingernails digging into her palms in her attempts not to push the shower away. Adjusting her footing against the tray Jess tried to deflect the relentless stream of water for a moment, but it was to no avail, for Miss Sarah simply moved the shower head with her.

Just as her right nipple began to burn, and her whimpers turned to cries, Miss Sarah changed position again, dropping the shower's rose to just above Jess's nub. 'How sensitive is it down there?' Miss Sarah moved the spray function lower, but avoiding the clerk's clit. 'I guess you're still pretty turned on from Madam's visit.'

Clamping her lips tighter, Jess said nothing.

'Madam's hands must have felt good against your tits.' Miss Sarah stared directly into Jess's eyes, mentally challenging her to look away. 'She has such soft skin, doesn't she?'

As Miss Sarah spoke she moved the shower heat closer, so the water beat harder against the small triangle of pubic hair. Jess could virtually feel Madams hands pinching her flesh.

'I bet you wanted her to lick them, run her hot little tongue over your squeezed teats.' Still keeping the shower head steady, Miss Sarah's eyes gleamed with the thrill of control. 'Or maybe you wanted her to take her mouth lower. Perhaps you pictured yourself sitting over her face, her teeth nibbling at your pussy, your juice dripping down her chin.'

Jess, who'd been far too engrossed in what was happening to have thought about that at the time, now had that gloriously sexy image firmly implanted in her head, just as Miss Sarah had intended.

Despite the practice she'd had during her exercise sessions Jess's legs and arms were beginning to ache with the effort of staying still, and as her soaking hair dripped down her neck, goose pimples broke out on her shoulders. The contrast in temperatures between the top and lower parts of her body was only relieved by the rising steam. The combination of upper-body chill, the intense heat pounding just off her nub, and her desperation to come made Jess begin to quake.

'Not yet, young lady.' Miss Sarah lowered the shower to Jess's feet. 'You need to understand the reasons behind Madam's desire before you are allowed to come … if I allow you to come.'

Blinking her watering eyes Jess clenched her toes in the effort not to move away from the stinging spray.

'Get out.'

The sudden cessation of the deluge was as big a shock to Jess as its initial presence. Picking up a large bath sheet, Miss Sarah knelt before Jess and began to dry her from the feet up. She moved slowly, making sure she both towelled and inflamed the girl's sensitive skin at the same time.

Jess's mind surged as she reviewed the reality of the

situation. All that was happening was that she was being dried after an intensive shower, and yet every square centimetre of her was on fire. It was as if at any second her craving for a climax, for any sort of release at all, would overwhelm her. She gritted her teeth. She had to win this. She had to, even if she wasn't sure why.

As Miss Sarah reached her knees, Jess couldn't shake the picture of Madam licking her out, and privately cursed the mistress for adding to the cocktail of erotic scenarios that tussled in her head.

At last the towel was draped around her lower back, and Jess took a sharp intake of breath as she prepared for her pussy to be dried. An act she knew could be her undoing, her failure, but as the drips of water across her arse were soaked up, Miss Sarah dabbed the wet skin all around the mound, but left it untouched.

Much to Miss Sarah's amusement, Jess groaned out loud. It was so predictable. She should have known what Miss Sarah had planned, and yet she'd hoped for some contact so badly.

Speeding up, Miss Sarah wiped Jess's stomach, neck and shoulders, before dropping the bath sheet, leaving the clerk's breasts and crotch damp and chilled. Standing back, crossing her arms over her uniform the mistress said, 'I admit it. I'm impressed. I thought you'd have come by now.'

Jess wasn't sure how to react. It had sounded like a compliment, but the look on Miss Sarah's face told a different story. She was obviously more annoyed than ever at Jess's unexpected levels of self-control.

'You need to understand Madam's fantasy.' She grabbed Jess's right wrist and pulled her into the tiny bedroom. Throwing her down onto the shiny chocolate-coloured duvet, Miss Sarah wasted no time in positioning

Jess as Madam had been. Her hands stretched across the bed above her head, her knees bent, her ankles pressed awkwardly against her thighs.

Jess braced herself for the addition of bindings, but Miss Sarah smiled sardonically at the clerk's obvious expectation. 'Oh no, Miss Sanders, we have to be stronger than our clients. We have to be ice. Not only must we *never* show weakness, or personal want, we must have the strength of mind not to be bound. Our willpower alone has to be enough to keep us in one position while our bodies receive what we so badly desire, or sometimes what we don't desire but are instructed to receive.'

'But I'm just the accommodation clerk!' Jess's voice both pleaded and sighed with defeat as the realisation hit her. How had she been so slow to see this? She wasn't just the clerk any more, and now, as she lay huddled on the soft bed, her body un-tethered, and yet voluntarily remaining in the position Miss Sarah dictated, Jess knew she was in far too deep to ever walk out of this bizarre hotel.

She'd known it from the first day, she'd known it as she stared blankly at the job paper the night before, but this was the first time she'd admitted it to herself. Lee was right. She did need this. Jess experienced a strange mix of humiliation and defeat as the knowledge of the untold gratification to come begin to knot in her stomach.

Although she hadn't voiced her thoughts, Miss Sarah's self-satisfied grin told Jess she had sensed her air of capitulation. 'You may make noise, but you may not talk. You will not come until permission is given. You will not move.'

Jess managed to resist the temptation to speak as her colleague produced a fresh speculum, and pulled on some latex gloves.

Now she knew why Miss Sarah had been so keen for her to witness the intrusion Madam had so willingly paid for. Having seen how stretched her channel was about to become, knowing how painful it would feel, how empty she would be, was a clever way of winning psychological points off Jess.

Although she stayed in position, Jess was unable to prevent her shoulders from quaking, as fear at what she was about to experience engulfed her.

Jess wished she couldn't see the triumphant look on Miss Sarah's face as she oozed lube between her fingers. 'I suggest you relax Miss Sanders.'

Inhaling a steady low breath and closing her eyes against what was to come. She pictured Madam licking her out; focusing on how proud she would feel after this was over, when she had succeeded in taking all that Miss Sarah could throw at her.

The cold cream made Jess flinch as a medically scented finger probed around her pussy, easing itself up inside her. Instantly her body reacted to the longed for pressure of something filling her hole. A sharp slap from Miss Sarah across her tits made Jess determined to concentrate all the harder, as the digit glided in and out of her, making a far more protracted job of lubing her channel than Madam had endured.

Gritting her teeth, Jess let out a small moan of frustration as, just as she'd convinced her brain to not allow her to come, but to accept the tension rising within her, Miss Sarah withdrew her hand, and the abrupt emptiness was unbearable.

It was short-lived however, for within seconds the sterile metal tool was at the entrance of her vagina, and being pushed firmly inside. Gulping back the yell of 'Fuck!' that began to rise from her lips as she remembered Miss Sarah's no talking rule, Jess stiffened her muscles as the cool metal slid inside her, widening her passage as it moved.

Keeping her arms still was a virtually impossible mission, as the instinct to knock Miss Sarah's hands from her became intense. Jess clenched her palms together as she had seen Madam do, but was all too aware there would be no young assistant to come and distract her by putting their tits into her willing hands.

Miss Sarah gave the speculum a final push, and Jess squealed as the last stretch of the metal arms opened. Taking some deep breaths, Jess tried to distract herself from how open she was, but the air that ran around her insides only went to remind her how nothing would be entering her now; nothing would be filling her up.

Silently praying that Miss Sarah would begin to lick her clit as she had Madam, Jess wriggled against the bed, trying to unknot the muscles that were freezing her shoulders into a stiff mass.

With one hand holding the instrument in place, Miss Sarah rose from her crouched position at the end of the bed and stared dispassionately at Jess, a look which belied the tightness of her breasts beneath her costume. Reaching under her bed she produced two small silver objects that Jess took to be bulldog clips.

'If you remember, Miss Sanders, I informed you that to truly succeed in our work we have to go further than our clients, experience more, and cope better.'

Eyes wide with horror, she watched as Miss Sarah leant forward, and with a preliminary pinch of her right nipple, snapped the clip over her teat. The clerk screamed as the foreign object bit into her flesh, her pink tip protruding from its top. Before Jess had time to adjust to the new pain, Miss Sarah repeated the process, and a second nipple clamp was digging its teeth cruelly into her.

Automatically, Jess went to raise her arms, to rid herself of the relentless sting, but Miss Sarah had been expecting the move, and spoke sharply, 'If you move now, you will have failed.'

Instantly, Jess dropped her hands again, whimpering with the combined ache of staying in one position for so long, and the flushing of her abused tits.

Speaking with almost nauseating sweetness, Miss Sarah said, 'I'm sure Mrs Peters will be pleased when she hears you can take the nipple clamps and the speculum at the same time.'

Jess squeezed her eyes closed. All she sensed was an intense hurt, a squealing throb in her muscles, and a yearning for an orgasm that somehow overrode all of that.

Saying nothing, Miss Sarah dropped from sight. Jess tensed further, waiting for something to happen, but nothing did. The seconds ticked by, and no other part of her was touched. Her tits burnt, but she was surprised to find she was adjusting to the anguish. She only knew that Miss Sarah was still there by the relentless presence of the speculum being held in place.

Just as she'd begun to think nothing would happen, and despair gripped her, a slow tongue ran over her clit.

Jess's back arched and her fingers and toes clenched against themselves, as her body went into instant unstoppable overload.

The speculum was hastily removed, and Jess yelled out against its loss as the metal clattered to the floor. Instantly Miss Sarah began to twist and tweak at the nipple clamps, sending fresh waves of agony through Jess's captured breasts.

Stunting Jess's shrieks, Miss Sarah brought her lips to hers, kissing her with an angry fervour that Jess was happy to reciprocate.

Whispering through her kisses, Miss Sarah said, 'You may move your arms, but not your legs.'

Ignoring the crack they made as she moved them far too fast after such a period of inactivity, Jess brought her hands to Miss Sarah's chest and pinched it hard through the nurse's uniform, wishing that the sticky fabric wasn't there so she could see her superior's magnificent chest properly.

Dropping her mouth to Jess's tits, Miss Sarah began to flick her tongue over and around the clamps, filling Jess with the strangest mix of pleasure and suffering that she'd ever experienced.

It was too much. Her pussy, empty and neglected, began to pulse and clench as if it were full, and her nipples sent tremors of lust through every inch of her body as, without waiting for the permission she was sure she needed, Jess's tormented frame jacked against her boss, coming in a violent shout of relief.

Sweat poured from Jess as she finally lay still against the bed. She couldn't believe she'd just done that, and she wasn't ready to admit she'd sort of enjoyed it, or how badly she had wanted to strip the uniform from her superior's body.

'Look at me, Miss Sanders.' Miss Sarah spoke more softly now.

Jess looked; a shameful expression on her face.

'Don't look like that. You succeeded, you survived.'

'But I came without permission, and I ...' Jess's voice dropped so it was barely audible. '... I didn't think my body could do things like that.'

Miss Sarah flashed an unexpectedly kind smile, but rather than comment she changed the subject. 'So, do you understand why Madam likes that? Why such total lack of control and the denial of what she wants most turns her on?'

Jess thought carefully before she replied, 'Because she is usually always in control of her life?'

'Good,' Miss Sarah inclined her head. 'If you understand why the clients come here, then you'll be better at this than if you don't.'

A sharply pointed fingernail trailed slowly across Jess's cheek. 'I'm beginning to think Mrs Peters might be right about you.'

Jess was unable to keep the pleading tone from her voice. 'But *what* about me, *what is it*?'

'You already know the answer to that, Miss Sanders. Now, I have to change and get ready for my next visitor, and you have work to do in the office.' A flash of regret shone in her eyes. 'Shame really, 'cause I think I'd like to have taken things further.'

'Further?' Jess winced as she rose from her place on the bed, trying hard to comprehend that Miss Sarah was now being nice to her, all jealousy apparently gone. *Had that been an act? Another means of testing her?*

Miss Sarah ignored the questioning inflection in Jess's voice, simply repeating, 'Go and shower, Miss Sanders, before you return to your office. The rest will do you good. I have organised another exercise session for you tonight, and then again tomorrow morning. I'll see you then.'

Chapter Eleven

'YOU'VE VISITED THE SCHOOL room, the study and the medical bay.'

Jess sat at her computer terminal and nodded meekly at Mrs Peters. Her body was stiff and warm from the mile Miss Sarah had forced her to cycle on the exercise bike, with the love balls once again tucked firmly inside her channel. Every time Jess had been close to climax, Miss Sarah had slapped her chest and she'd felt uncomfortably unfulfilled, a situation not improved by the capricious way her boss was now staring at her.

'Miss Sarah tells me you successfully helped her to entertain a client yesterday; a guest who has not always taken kindly to a change from her usual routine. I also hear that you are adjusting to your new exercise schedule.' Mrs Peters spoke with such lack of expression that Jess wasn't sure if she was being complimented, chastised, or if the manageress was merely making an observation. 'I have a very important visitor due here tonight, Miss Sanders, and I intend for him to meet you.'

The butterflies that seemed to live in Jess's stomach these days began to flutter as she listened.

'The outcome of this evening will determine many things about the future direction of life on the fifth floor, including your own. Much has been made of your natural submission and I think the reality of that has begun to sink in with you. The question is, are you good enough to stay on my staff? Do you have what it takes? I did wonder if I'd have to ask if you wanted to stay, but from the evidence of Miss Sarah, from Lee, and from the recordings I have made of you, I am convinced that you have already crossed the point of no return. So the real question is will I let you stay?

An unexpected panic gripped Jess. It hadn't occurred to her that she might not be allowed to stay. She was further disconcerted by the knowledge of what that panic meant. And, on top of that, she wondered just how many recordings had been made of her since she arrived. All the secret but necessary sessions she'd had in the Ladies, the conversation with Lee in the staff room, her encounter with Madam, her sessions in the gym ... Jess shook her head, trying not to remember how good all that had felt.

'I can see you're thinking carefully about what I've said.' Mrs Peters' features remained immobile, but Jess couldn't help feel as if she was being mocked in some way. 'Before you meet my special guest, I need to reassure myself that you're capable of coping with a wider range of challenges.'

Saying nothing, Jess kept her eyes trained on the keyboard, over which her fingers remained frozen in mid-sentence.

'I have arranged for you to meet one of my regulars. You will accompany me now.'

'But I'm needed here ...' Jess gestured to the pile of work that awaited her fractured concentration.

'It can wait.' Mrs Peters pulled back her shoulders and stepped away from the desk so Jess could stand up. 'We really must do something about your wardrobe, child.'

Jess looked at the suit she'd bought for her new job at the hotel. Smart black skirt and jacket, with a crisp fitting white blouse beneath. She couldn't see what was wrong with it.

'Oh your appearance is fine for the office, Miss Sanders,' Mrs Peters continued, once again giving Jess the impression she could read her mind, 'but as a member of my more exclusive staff, you should dress more appropriately.'

Images of stockings, Basques, tight fitting dresses and PVC nurse's outfits swam in Jess's head.

'You need to give in, you know. Every now and then I think you have, but then you start the struggle with your conscience all over again.' Mrs Peters lifted Jess's chin with two of her slender fingers and peered into her eyes. 'The more you fight what that lively little body of yours truly desires, the harder you will find your life here.'

'I…' Much to her relief, Jess's sentence was cut short by the arrival of the lift, as she hadn't really known what she'd been going to say.

The atmosphere of the stuffy lift became increasingly uncomfortable as the two women ascended to the fifth floor. Only once the silver doors had opened, and Mrs Peters had stepped into the narrow hallway that ran between the five main doors of the hotel's top level, did she began to explain her intentions.

'My client has rearranged his business appointments today specifically because I have asked for his assistance in your instruction.'

A lump developed in Jess's throat as she listened.

'He calls himself David Proctor, his real name is of no consequence. He is less formal than many of the guests we have here, and prefers to be referred to by his Christian name.'

'May I ask what room he uses, Mrs Peters?' This was the first time Jess had ever asked her employer a direct question, and she wasn't at all sure how her request for information would be received.

'You may ask.' Mrs Peters considered her pupil for a moment. 'You were wise to ask for permission for that information. Again you prove to me how quickly you can catch on to the rules here.' Her eyes narrowed as she surveyed the clerk. 'I'd like you to remove your blouse and underwear, and then I'll tell you what you need to know.'

Jess slid her jacket from her shoulders, and holding it clumsily between her knees, unbuttoned her white top, painfully aware of how blatantly her nipples were protruding as she removed her bra, and how damp her knickers were as she slid them to the floor.

'Now, slip your jacket back on and do it up. I'll take your clothes.'

Mrs Peters held the garments as though they were offensive articles, before pointing to the furthest door on the right side of the corridor. There were only two rooms Jess hadn't visited so far, and she was fairly confident it wouldn't be the secret room she'd heard about on her arrival at Fables. So it had to be the dungeon. A gut wrenching churning began in her stomach.

'The fact you've gone rather pale, tells me you've worked out which room this is. An excellent place to teach you the finer points of satisfying our visitors. Master Philips is particularly fond of it in there.' Mrs Peters took Jess's hand. Her skin was cold, and yet still managed to send a bolt of heat through Jess's nervous system.

Tugged and guided into the room with only the token resistance of uncertainty, Jess allowed herself a few moments to take in the contents of Room 50. The subdued light provided by wall candles, cast strange shadows after the bright glare of the lift and corridor.

More than usually aware of her breathing, Jess felt it scrape in her throat as she took in the focal point of the room. The rack, which she could easily imagine Lee enjoying as Mrs Peters had indicated, loomed menacing and silent. The walls were hung with sinister-looking meat hooks holding every torture and correction implement possible.

In contrast to all the other rooms in the hotel, the dungeon was neither air-conditioned nor spotless. Dust had been allowed to accumulate on the floor; there was no evidence of any form of heating. The overall impression of medieval dankness that the architect of the room had tried to secure could certainly be declared a success.

'Some of our guests require us to dress the part in this room. Medieval tunics, wench outfits, slaves tatters, and so on. Others couldn't care less what we wear as long as it comes off quickly and they get the kicks they've paid for.'

Her eyes wide, Jess continued to survey the room as Mrs Peters spoke.

'David likes business suits and no underwear, but with one medieval addition.' Mrs Peters went over to a wooden cabinet in the corner of the room, returning with a slim belt that had a wide flap of leather attached halfway along its length. Without having to be told, Jess knew exactly what she was looking at and her mind immediately recoiled at the idea of the chastity belt.

'Hurry up, girl, let's get it on you, he'll be here in a minute. Lift your skirt, I need to put this around your waist, and believe me, you'd be very uncomfortable if I hurried and placed it incorrectly.'

Deftly, Mrs Peters fastened the belt around Jess's waist, commenting as she did so on how much more toned her stomach muscles were, although she also added that there was still room for improvement. Pushing a hand between her clerk's legs, she grabbed the oval of leather, which had been lined with sheepskin, and pulled it firmly over Jess's pussy, attaching it securely to the front of the belt with a silver clamp.

Unable to contain a frustrated moan as her snatch was teased and incarcerated by the furry strap, Jess squirmed against its tickling surface.

'Miss Sanders, I wish you to listen very carefully to what I have to say.' Mrs Peters' voice was like steel as she twisted the clerk around to face her. 'David will be here in a moment. You will do what he says, when he says, without question, but you have to start things. This is your session, but I will be watching, assessing your handling of the situation.'

'My session?'

'Yours.'

'But,' Jess stammered as she struggled to comprehend what was being demanded of her, 'I'm a submissive, or so you keep saying. I don't do controlling.'

'And yet you will do this,' The manageress's fingers danced lightly over Jess's naked cleavage, sending a cruel extra gush of longing down her spine. 'I think you will understand once you and David get into your stride.'

'I …' Jess's pointless protests were interrupted by a sharp rap at the door.

'Let him in, Miss Sanders.'

There was no time to argue. It was as if her body was operating outside of her brain, as if she was watching herself invite the client into the room on autopilot, propelled by an internal desire-fuelled curiosity to find out what was going to happen next.

A mute greeting between Mrs Peters and Mr Proctor

increased the uneasy yet expectant mood in the room, as Jess found herself hovering before the man, not really sure what to do next. He was regarding her with expressionless round green eyes, set in a circular face. Neither fat nor thin, the customer would have summed up the terms "average build and average height" perfectly. His slightly greying foppish hair hung over one side of his face, and a hand kept lifting it up to knock it away. About 45 years old Jess guessed, with an expensive designer suit that indicated he was on his lunch hour from some high powered employment.

After Jess had failed to move for several moments, Mrs Peters gave an exasperated sigh. 'Honestly, girl, have you paid no attention to Miss Sarah when she starts a session?' She turned to David, her accent gentle and kind, at total odds with the way she had addressed Jess. 'My apologies. As I explained on the phone, she is very new.'

The client, his face revealing nothing, nodded.

'David likes his experiences in the dungeon to start with the mistress in charge ordering him to strip off, and, as this is a dungeon, punished. I would have thought that would be obvious.'

Feeling a failure before she'd even started, and smarting from the unfairness of the situation, Jess's face coloured violently in embarrassment. She'd never told anyone to do anything in her life, and she wasn't sure she could now.

Summoning all her courage, and doing her best to picture how Miss Sarah acted in her mistress role, Jess said, 'Strip.' Despite her attempt to sound masterful, her voice came out rather squeakily. The client however, remained solemn, and obeyed, his suit hitting the dirty floor with considerable speed.

An unexpected jolt of power ran through Jess as she

observed the man humble before her. His cock was proud and firm, asking for attention all on its own, while his untanned skin showed evidence of previous beatings at the tops of his legs, back and arse. Doing her best to adopt an expression of haughty disdain, Jess circled David slowly, just as Mrs Peters had done to her in the past.

Increasingly conscious of the belt beneath her skirt Jess wondered how long she could leave it before taking off her own clothes, and allow David see that she wore the belt for him beneath. Not yet, she judged, and turning from him collected a paddle from a nearby hook. With her heart pounding, Jess ordered the guest onto his hands and knees.

The speed at which he capitulated gave Jess a further buzz, which in turn made her chest swell and her pussy clench.

Standing behind him, she found herself shaking as she swung her arm back to administer the first blow. Halfway through uncertainty swamped her. *What if I hit him too hard? What if I damage him?* Consequently, when the paddle connected with David's skin, it barely even touched him.

'You're not swatting flies, girl.' Mrs Peters' disapproval cut through Jess like a knife. 'Again, and mean it!'

Stung, and yet strangely boosted, by her boss's words, Jess stared hard at the waiting butt before her and aimed again. This time the smack echoed through the room, making David cry out and rock forwards on his hands. 'Keep still!' Jess roared the words, taking everyone, including herself, by surprise, a frisson of satisfaction ripping through her at the expression in Mrs Peters' eyes as she did so. A look that, just for a second, flashed with a private concern that swamped any satisfaction at the clerk's obedience.

Two strikes later and David's cries had altered to controlled whimpers of pain, which Jess realised to her horror, she'd actively enjoyed inflicting. Lowering her hand, she dropped the paddle to the floor, and ran her fingers over the deep pink welts she'd created on his arse. Jess felt his flesh react to her touch, his heavy breathing the predominant sound in the room, as she swapped her fingers for her tongue, running its moist warmth around the circumference of the fast bruising lines.

All the time Jess was becoming more aware of the belt stroking her, of the sheepskin, no longer soft and fluffy, but matted and sodden with her juices. Her hands itched to tear off her suit, to stop the polyester of her jacket buffing her bullet nipples, to yank away her skirt, and to replace the strap with the cock that wavered in the air before her.

Continuing to lick the client's arse, Jess slipped a hand between his legs. David's long drawn out groan broke the spell that had weaved itself around the room, and Mrs Peters words dripped acid as she called out, 'I admire your technique, child, but this is a *dungeon*. Punishment must ALWAYS come before reward here; don't you agree, David?'

The man moaned, and still suffering from the withdrawal of the unexpected stimulation he'd been receiving, replied meekly, 'Whatever you say, Mrs Peters.'

Hesitating, the manageress remembered her position, and with a brittle voice said, 'However, you are the customer, if you which Miss Sanders to continue with her *unusual* approach to chastisement, I shall not stop her.'

David stood, brushing his dusty hands together, his face still crimson from where blood had rushed to his head 'No, I agreed to help in this child's instruction, so if you wish a more punishment-based lesson, then perhaps we should tell her more about what we expect of her.'

Jess hardly dared breathe; she'd never heard anyone talk to Mrs Peters like that before, let alone question her decisions, but she simply smiled. It was not a nice smile. 'You are quite correct, David. It seems that Jess needs no assistance in following her instincts to pleasure a man, but punishment and instruction – well, there's room for improvement there, I think.'

'Quite so, Mrs Peters.' The client's eyes roamed across the girl, shining with the greed he'd previously kept under wraps . 'Is she wearing the device as requested?'

'She is.'

'Well then, I think we'll overlook this interlude and carry on as planned.' David and Mrs Peters exchanged knowing looks.

The mistress inclined her head thoughtfully. 'I concede that I should have perhaps informed Miss Sanders a bit more about what to do, but I was curious to see what she would do without that guidance.'

'I can understand that.'

Continuing as though Jess wasn't in the room, Mrs Peters said, 'I confess I was concerned that Miss Sanders would get a taste for correction, and I'd lose her submissive skills. You have helped put my mind at rest. Thank you, David.'

Nausea built in Jess's throat as she listened, forcing her to swallow.

'Right.' Mrs Peters clapped her hands together. 'Let's get on with this, Miss Sanders. The session should have progressed with you smacking Mr Proctor until he begged you to stop. Then, he would have turned the tables on you; reverting you to your usual more submissive role. I can't tell you how, as that is his decision and he changes the session a little each time. I think that is a simple enough premise – even for you.'

Jess's hackles rose, but she bit back the uncharacteristic retort that was building within her. If Mrs Peters was trying to make her angry by suggesting she was not only a toy, but was stupid as well, then it was working, but she'd be damned if she'd give her the satisfaction of letting her know she was getting to her.

'An additional penalty may be required.' Mr Proctor sounded hopeful as he spoke.

'Well, I did promise I'd make this training session worth your while,' Mrs Peters replied solemnly. 'And how else is she going to learn?'

I really am just a thing. A toy; something to play with and then put back in my office type box until they want to amuse themselves again. It was a sobering thought, and one that, now it had arrived Jess couldn't shift as she was bodily repositioned behind a crouching David, the paddle pushed back into her hand.

Swinging the weapon back, her brain continued to race, making her deaf to her target's cries. *You are nothing here.* SMACK. *They will use you up.* SMACK. Jess didn't register David when he asked her to stop. She kept on hitting him, again and again as a more frightening inner voice added, *You like it!* SMACK. *You need it!* SMACK. *Lee was right ...*

The orders from David for her to stop, had morphed into pleading and begging, and finally they sank into her consciousness.

Jess lowered her arm, aware that she was exhausted. No one moved. Jess couldn't believe how soundly she'd been spanking the smarting arse that virtually shone before her. David had sunk to the ground, his arms collapsed beneath him. The clerk kept expecting Mrs Peters' disapproval to boom around the room, but no one spoke.

Her eyes glued to her feet, Jess waited, terrified of what might happen next, yet impatient for it to begin, more aware than ever of the insistent pressure of the chastity belt.

It was the slight movement of David's feet that unfroze the moment. With a guttural groan he eased himself upwards, swaying a little as he stood. 'Look at me.'

Jess's blood froze in her veins, as she met the client's gaze.

'No ... one ...' he paced his words slowly as if he was still struggling for control of his breath, '...has ever treated me in that way. No one *ever* disobeys my requests.'

'I ... I'm sorry.'

'You will be.' David turned to Mrs Peters, a barely suppressed anger bubbling in his words. 'You were worried she'd get a taste for correction. Well I don't think you can relax on that front yet, but if a hefty punishment always follows her slips into acts of dominance, perhaps her taste for a more assertive role can be quashed. As you're here, I wonder if you'd oblige me.'

'Certainly.' It was the first word Mrs Peters had uttered since Jess had finished using the paddle and Jess was glad she couldn't see the expression that went with her tone.

David took a step nearer to Jess. 'While I consider how to proceed, I wonder if you would remove that awful suit from her, and then increase the effect of the belt.'

'Of course.'

Still unwilling to face her boss, Jess closed her eyes against the latest humiliation, as she continued to try and stop the voices in her head telling her this is what she actually wanted. Standing limp as Mrs Peters ripped the clothes from her, the clerk stiffened as a rough probing finger jabbed its way beneath the sheepskin band.

'Just as I suspected! The girl has no self-control. This strap is soaked through.'

A cruel gleam came to the client's eyes. 'I suggest an insert.'

His words made Jess's eyes spring back open. *What sort of insert?*

'Open your eyes!' Mrs Peters held a small, perfectly polished, wooden dildo in the palm of her hand. 'You will bend your knees and crouch down.'

Jess moved reluctantly, the constricting of her lower body increasing the tension that rippled across her pussy. Once positioned, the manageress ordered her to stay exactly where she was.

For the first time Jess was glad of all the training Miss Sarah had been giving her during her enforced exercise classes at keeping still and holding uncomfortable positions for long periods of time.

Manhandling Jess's crotch, Mrs Peters loosened the strap and then, without ceremony, pushed the dildo up inside her, making her yelp as it filled her cramped channel to the hilt, and remained trapped there, hard and unyielding, by the strap.

'Fasten that belt extra tight, Mrs Peters.' David was now sufficiently recovered to prowl around as Mrs Peters yanked at the belt until it dug into Jess's stomach, and the dildo was pushed in even deeper.

Her knees were beginning to tremble as Jess waited, too scared to move now that the wood was firmly inside her.

'Why so worried?' Mrs Peters taunted as she rose to

her feet, 'I'm sure you wanted to have something in that hot little pussy, and now you have. Some gratitude wouldn't go amiss.'

Through gritted teeth, Jess said, 'Thank you, Mrs Peters.'

'That's better. Honestly, if you can't mange basic politeness then there's no way you'll progress with us. You won't meet my guest and you certainly won't discover what's behind the door to Room 54. Now, over to you, David.'

Jess watched him with morbid fascination, as the dildo shifted slightly within her, pussy juice escaping from the sponge of the strap.

'Stand up and approach.'

Jess moved awkwardly, clumsy with the solid shaft within her.

'I would like you to lie here.'

For a second Jess felt as though her heart had stopped beating as he pointed towards the rack, but then realised he was gesturing to a thin bench just behind it. Unsure if it would be wide enough to support her, but not wanting to provoke any more anger, Jess obeyed.

Her head rested on the hard surface, but it was so narrow her shoulders and hips protruded over the edge, and it was very difficult not to let her legs drop over either side of the bench. That problem was quickly solved however, when David told her to put her feet on the floor, which forced her into a position where her belt dug deeper into her flesh and the dildo stretched her channel further.

Unsure what do to with her arms, she crossed them over her chest, only to have them irritably knocked away. 'I want to see those tits, girl. Give me your wrists.' David took both arms in one hand and placed them over and above her head, pulling one to each side of the bench tying them to the legs with a scratchy piece of rope, leaving Jess vulnerable, stretched, and helpless. She might as well have been put on the rack after all.

'Very pretty don't you think, Mrs Peters?'

'Indeed. I was only saying to Miss Sarah the other day how much potential she has, and if Miss Sanders has any sense at all, she won't allow herself to come until she is given permission to do so.'

You see, you're just a toy. Jess tried to block out her thoughts, concentrating instead on not climaxing around the insistent presence of the chastity belt and plug.

David swung a leg over the bench and stood astride Jess. The intoxicating aroma of sex hung around his cock. It was unbelievably tight and flecks of precome were dotted at its head. Then, David sat on Jess's stomach, winding her, his backside adding extra pressure to her already desperate cunt, her clit contracting against the strap.

She'd guessed what was about happen a second before it did. As his cock was guided into her dry mouth, and his hands began an all out assault against her breasts, she forced herself to calm her breath.

As his fingers tweaked her nipples urgently, he raised his legs slightly and pushed his groin forward, making Jess open her throat wider so she didn't choke against him. He moved faster and faster, and Jess had to battle to relax enough not to gag.

Every time David rocked forward his legs pressed harder to Jess's sides, the wooden dick juddered within her, and the strap sent shockwaves of insistent pleasure through her snatch.

Unable to move, her body drenched in sweat, her red hair plastered to her head, Jess could feel David was reaching his own limits, and with a final shove forwards, he pinched her nipples with brutal fingers, causing her to scream out against the spunk that shot into her mouth.

It was too much. How was anyone supposed to withstand so much physical attention and not come? Jess tried to rein in the climax she felt rip through her, but it was pointless, and despite David's weight as he crashed back against her torso, her back arched and her legs and arms shook, the rope cutting into her wrists as she bellowed out her body-wracking defeat.

Chapter Twelve

THEY HAD BEEN WAITING for her to fail. The proof of that had been all too obvious in the sickeningly satisfied way both Mrs Peters and Mr Proctor swiftly cut her arms free and, with trickles of sperm still running from the corners of her mouth, had yanked her upright so fast her head spun.

Seconds later Jess had found herself achingly empty as the wooden dildo was removed and the sodden sheepskin strap was replaced with a dry one, keeping up the pressure on her soaking snatch.

It was very quiet now. Jess wasn't sure how long it had been since anyone had touched her, but guessed it was a good half an hour. David had left with regretful comments about having to return to work and missing the penalty the clerk would have to endure for coming without permission. The manageress, however, had been quick to reassure him that she would film the proceedings so he could watch at a later date.

Jess knew Mrs Peters was still in the room, but although she occasionally heard her moving around behind her, the thick padded strap that held her neck in place prohibited her from turning her head.

The neck strap was her only restraint, but it was all that was needed to keep Jess firmly tethered to a wooden post she'd previously assumed was part of the medieval scenery, but now realised was a crude attempt at a pillory. Shifting her bare feet against the dusty floor sent fresh waves of longing through her tormented pussy, her forbidden orgasm long forgotten by her hungry body. She had cried for a while, but all that had achieved was to release some of the tension of the previous session, and now she could feel stiff streaks across her cheeks where the tears had dried.

She was terribly thirsty, but a more pressing need was concerning her. Her bladder was incredibly full, but Jess didn't dare ask for permission to use the bathroom. She tried to contract her stomach to stop any urine leaking from her; not wanting to consider what might happen if she wet herself.

Her eyelids were almost as heavy as her bladder, and Jess had to fight to keep her eyes open, fearful that if she drifted into even a gentle doze, her body would relax and her bladder would empty of its own accord.

Footsteps told Jess that Mrs Peters was approaching at last. Facing her trainee, she held a large glass of water and a drinking straw. Jess tried and failed to shake her head within the confines of her restraint. There was no way she could risk drinking anything without disgracing herself.

Pointedly ignoring the clerk's blatant distress, Mrs Peters placed the straw in the glass and brought it to the girl's lips. 'You must be very thirsty by now, Miss Sanders.'

'I'm fine, thank you.'

'But you must keep up your fluids, I'm sure Miss Sarah has told you as much during your exercise sessions.'

Struggling not to start crying, or even to beg her boss to take the glass away, Jess said, 'Really, I'm fine, thank you.'

'And yet you will drink.' Mrs Peters grabbed Jess's chin, pulled her jaw down and shoved the straw between the newly parted lips. 'You will drink it all.'

'I can't I'll …'

'You can and you will.'

Jess took a tiny reluctant suck, and felt the wonderfully fresh water glide down her sandpaper dry throat.

'More.'

The conflict between Jess's desire to drink, and her bladder's incapability of holding more liquid was driving Jess mad. With Mrs Peters standing over her, however, she had no choice. Taking the glass in her trembling hands, she gulped down the chilled water before pushing the empty cup back at Mrs Peters, who walked away. Clenching every muscle in her body, and clamping her eyes shut, Jess was determined not to humiliate herself until the last possible moment.

Again she could hear Mrs Peters moving behind her, and then, suddenly her eyes flew open and a squeal of pain shot from her lips. Her right breast had been struck with a short black cane.

The mistress changed her attention to the left nipple, and with precision accuracy brought the weapon down, sending new streaks of agony through the clerk. Tensing her pelvic floor as much as humanly possible, Jess became more aware than ever of the sweat-sodden sheepskin between her legs.

Sensing victory, Mrs Peters began to alternate the agonising strikes with greater speed.

As each burning hit struck her, Jess felt both her control slipping away, and the chastity strap becoming more of an irritant then ever. On the sixth strike, her nipples soaring with pain, Jess screamed and her body went limp, all the fight knocked out of her in one go.

With a speed born of practice, Mrs Peters released the belt, making Jess yelp as the strap came away, its Velcro like pressure making her feel as if she was having a plaster ripped from her pussy. The restraints were also swiftly removed, and half carrying, half dragging the clerk, the manageress pushed Jess into the discreetly hidden washroom at the back of the dungeon.

Ten minutes later, her legs weak, her breath shallow, Jess re-emerged into Room 50. She was desperate to sink to the floor, to rest her wobbling legs, but she managed to stay upright. Convinced that her hasty removal to the bathroom had signalled failure, Jess's mind leapt ahead to what horrors Mrs Peters might punish her with next.

An unreadable expression met her gaze when she finally risked a glance at her boss. The cane was still firmly in her fist, but she appeared more satisfied than angry, a fact that only served to confuse Jess further.

Carefully placing the cane to one side, Mrs Peters steered her bemused clerk to a chair, sat her down, and widened her legs. Instantly Jess stiffened. She felt extremely sore and exhausted, and there was no way she could take any extra stimulation.

'Not to worry, child.' Mrs Peters tone was strangely soft, as a hand soothed the raw skin at the top of Jess's thigh. 'This will help, I promise.'

A tongue began to lap away the mixture of liquids around Jess's channel, and a gentle hand stroked her chest, avoiding the tender tips where, only moments before, the same hand had inflicted such pain.

Sighing, Jess slouched a little further back, sliding closer to the expert tongue, which began to move faster, lighting her flesh, and charging her with a new energy. Her hands came up automatically, trailing through Mrs Peters' hair, and down her shoulders. As a finger found

Jess's hole, and the tonguing increased, she cried out, her body jacking against the wood. With her fingers still tangled in her boss's hair, Jess sank back, more sated than she'd ever been.

She could have slept then and there, but was aware of Mrs Peters' voice, coming as if from far away, and forced herself to remain vaguely conscious. At some point Lee must have arrived, for he was carrying her, and placing her on a wonderfully soft bed. Mrs Peters was telling her she'd performed well and although still needed instruction, would be meeting one of her special guest soon. Jess, however, wasn't sure if these congratulations were real or a dream, for she was already asleep.

Sam watched as the black cab pulled up outside his studio window. One of his neighbours had probably been shopping. Continuing to stare he saw a young man he vaguely recognised leave the car and head towards the main door of the apartment block, but Sam was still surprised when it was his intercom that buzzed.

'Mr Wheeler?'

'Yes?'

'I have a car waiting for you, sir.'

'Why? I'm not going anywhere?'

'I have my instructions, Mr Wheeler. You are to accompany me to the Fables Hotel.'

Sam took a hasty step back from the intercom. She'd sent a cab for him. A strange mixture of ego-fuelled self-satisfaction and uncertainty filled him as he glanced back out of the window at the figure below. He recognised him now. It was the barman and receptionist from the hotel. Laura Peters obviously didn't do the dirty work herself – well, apart from ... Sam tried hard to ignore the stirrings of his groin.

'Mr Wheeler?' A questioning voice crackled through the buzzer.

Coming to a split second decision, Sam said, 'Tell Mrs Peters that I thank her for the car, but am unable to accompany you for the moment as I have work to do. Perhaps she'd like to telephone me to arrange a more mutually convenient time?'

Sam wasn't sure how the emissary would respond to this, but he was convinced he shouldn't do what Laura wanted straight away, even though his dick was screaming at his brain to get to her as soon as possible.

'I have instructions to wait until it is convenient for you, sir.'

Sam sighed as static crackled over the intercom. 'And I imagine you are too sensible to disobey Mrs Peters' orders?'

'Yes, sir. I will await your company in the car.'

'But I could be hours, and it's already getting late.'

'Even so, I will wait.'

The artist glanced around the room, his gaze falling on his desk. It was clear. He'd finished the project he'd been working on an hour ago. Now he was trapped. Either he remained in the flat and pretended to work for a while, or he actually worked and made a start on his next project, or he gave in and went with Lee straight away. Hobson's choice.

If he stayed put Sam knew he'd simply pace the floor, his fantasies getting more and more lurid by the second. If he started a new work project, his concentration would be shot to pieces and he'd mess it up, and if he left now Laura would have won. Sam began to make coffee, his hands working independently from his brain, which was very much focused at cock level.

An hour. He'd make the car wait an hour, maybe even

two. How long should you make a dominatrix wait to show her you are definitely NOT her slave, but at the same time let her know you want to fuck her again, but not be punished for that desire? Two weeks ago even deliberating such a question would have felt absurd. Now it was a very real, albeit rather dangerous, dilemma.

Keeping out of sight of the window, Sam sipped the black liquid, not noticing that it was scalding. He thought again about what Laura had said, about him being her slave, about how the next time they met the rules would be stricter. *Surely she hadn't meant that? How could they be any stricter anyway?*

His coffee mug was empty, although Sam didn't actually remember drinking it. *This is ridiculous, who am I kidding?* He grabbed his overnight bag from its hiding place beneath the desk, took it into his bedroom, and stuffed enough inside to last for two nights away. After that, he'd have had enough of her, and he'd come home.

Chapter Thirteen

JESS WASN'T SURE WHAT time it was. Rolling onto her front, she winced as her bruised tits brushed the soft bedding.

'Good morning.'

Jess sat bolt upright.

Miss Sarah was observing her with her usual collected calm. 'Mrs Peters thought it best you be allowed to sleep in after your recent experiences. She did stress, however, that I should tell you this is a one-off. In future you will receive no exemption from your stated start time of employment at Fables, in whatever capacity.'

Heavy from her deep sleep, Jess said, 'Yes, Miss Sarah,' without really registering what her superior was saying.

'I trust you found my bed comfortable?'

'Your bed?' Looking around her properly for the first time Jess suddenly recognised the coffee-coloured duvet and the surroundings. 'I'm sorry, I didn't realise. I hope you haven't been inconvenienced.'

The other woman shrugged dismissively. 'I was entertaining an all night guest.'

Conscious of her naked chest, Jess pulled the duvet up over herself, making Miss Sarah snort with laughter. 'Honestly, I've seen it all before. Get up and shower, we need to squeeze an extra exercise session in before you get to your desk.'

'Yes, Miss Sarah.' Jess ached all over, the very last thing she wanted was exercise, but she was too tired to argue. It would be pointless anyway.

Jess let the shower jets soak into her, un-knotting the tension from her frame, and easing away the strain of the evening before. It had been strange, brutal even, but she knew, in a way she couldn't explain, that she'd enjoyed it. It had also been confusing. She simply could not work out the other women who worked on the fifth floor. Why did they take such delight in tormenting her, get so obsessed with punishing her when she failed to meet their over the top expectations, make out they hated her, and then in the next moment treat her with unexpected kindness? None of it made sense.

Reluctantly returning to the bedroom, wrapped in nothing but a huge bath sheet, Jess saw that Miss Sarah had prepared the room for the exercise session by pushing as much of the furniture back against the walls as possible.

'Your clothes were tracked down.' Miss Sarah gestured to a neatly folded pile on the stool near the dressing table. 'Come and stand over here.'

Moving slowly, Jess stood as instructed, just in front of the dominatrix.

'Now let's have that towel.' Miss Sarah took the bath sheet and stood back to critically examine the figure before her. 'Our work is paying off already. Your shape is improving almost daily. You've definitely lost that puppy fat you were clinging to, and your waist is trimmer.'

Feeling perversely pleased at the comments of the older woman, Jess kept still as Miss Sarah brought her hands to her breasts. 'And best of all,' Miss Sarah held her tits as if they were prized melons, 'we have managed to keep your chest its original size.'

Jess couldn't contain a sigh as her companion allowed the little finger of each hand to stray teasingly over her nipples.

'Down to business.' Miss Sarah clapped her hands and sat on her bedside stool. 'You will jog on the spot until I tell you to stop.'

'Please, Miss Sarah, I'm very tired, and I have so much work to catch up on, could we leave our exercises today? You did say I was doing well.'

'I did,' Miss Sarah's kind tone changed to one that bristled with disappointment, 'but we have targets to keep, child, and I believe you know as well as I do how unwise it is not to do as you are told here. Honestly, it's almost as if you have a taste for being chastised.'

Shocked that anyone should think she wanted their bizarre brand of discipline, and then wondering if perhaps Miss Sarah was right, Jess took a deep breath and, with a meek dip of her head began to jog on the spot.

'You see how delightfully her chest bounces as she jogs?'

Sam looked from Laura to the small screen in front of them and back again, trying to detect something more than professional appreciation in her voice, but failed. Determined to sound equally detached from the vision before him, he replied, 'She seems perfectly proportioned to me, why the fitness routine?'

'Miss Sanders has been encouraged in the belief that we are getting rid of her puppy fat, but really the routine is to instil in her a greater sense of discipline, obedience and stamina, all vital components in this job.'

Sam tried not to show his reaction as he witnessed, via the computer screen, the young girl being turned around and told to touch her toes. 'Her breasts and backside are rather bruised. Does that mean she isn't always as well behaved as this?'

'For a new girl she is doing well. But if you tell anyone I said that, there'll be trouble.' Laura got up from where she'd been sat, and stood behind her guest. His gorgeous torso was bare, and Laura couldn't resist running her hands over the toned flesh. He was still wearing his black combats, and Laura could see how hard his cock was beneath them.

On the screen before them, Jess's position had been altered again. sitting on the floor, her hands on her head, a look of total helplessness was etched on her face. 'Miss Sarah will sit down over the girl's legs now – yes, I thought so.' Laura spoke with the confidence of a boss satisfied with her workforce, 'This next exercise provides Miss Sanders with an incentive to keep going, however tired her body is.'

Sam watched, open mouthed, as Jess forced her tired frame up for the first sit up, close enough to Miss Sarah to be rewarded by a waiting tongue that lapped at the very tip of one breast. He didn't dare comment, and for the first time since he'd been escorted from the taxi directly to Laura Peters' private quarters, he felt his resolve to remain in mental control begin to slip.

He'd also been determined to stay in physical control, but that had been a battle Sam had lost almost immediately. Laura has been ready and waiting for him. Dressed in an exquisitely low cut green dress, her hair piled into a high ponytail, her feet bare, she had greeted him formally in Lee's presence. Once the barman had been dismissed however, the air in the room had positively prickled with static electricity. Her hands had come to his chest, and wasting no time in pulling off his shirt, she'd pushed him back onto a wooden seat. Tying his unresisting hands behind his back, Laura had explained there was something she'd like to show him. The "something" had turned out to be a film of Jess Sanders and the barman having a training session in the school room.

Sam wasn't sure how he hadn't come there and then at the sight of Laura on the screen, naked but for a billowing teacher's gown, orchestrating some very interesting S&M sex. Yet he was determined to prove to her, (and himself) that, despite being held captive by her yet again, he was no slave.

With the changing of the screen to show live coverage of Jess enduring a more physical workout, and the gentle pressure of Laura's fingers, Sam wasn't sure how much longer he could go without begging to have his cock released, sucked and fucked.

Although there was no sound coming from the webcam, Sam could tell that the new girl was panting, and he imagined groans and sighs coming from her mouth as she pushed her muscles harder just for the bliss of Miss Sarah's tongue on her chest. Eventually though, the clerk collapsed back, and Sam found he was holding his breath, willing her to get up and keep going. The sheen of sweat that glistened on her skin looked good enough to eat, and Sam felt her combined defeat and disappointment as Miss Sarah stood up, signalling the end of that exercise.

'Watch carefully. You'll like this bit.' Laura whispered in his ear, her breath tickling the sensitive skin of his neck, her right hand cupping his crotch and squeezing hard. 'I see you find Miss Sanders as fascinating as I do. This is good news.'

Sam watched as Miss Sarah produced a pair of love balls. They were obviously familiar to the girl, for she had parted her legs without being asked, and visibly clenched her teeth while the older woman took her time placing them inside her. Then, Jess was pulled to her feet and forced to stand with her arms outstretched and her legs apart.

'Her task is to stay perfectly motionless. The balls must not fall out, and she must not come, even though every inch of her must want to. It will require her to have excellent physical and mental discipline.'

Aware that his voice was rather more hoarse than usual, Sam asked, 'And if she fails and they fall out?'

'She'll face more correction.' Laura's eyes narrowed. 'Which reminds me, you are facing punishment for not accompanying Lee straight away.'

'Come off it, Laura! I do have a life you know. You can't snap your fingers and expect me to come running. And anyway, what do you call this if it isn't punishment?' Sam gestured the best he could in his captive state.

'Oh this is just fun, darling, but I tell you what; if you manage not to come before Jess does, then I'll forego the punishment I had planned for you, and you can help me administer it to her instead. OK?'

The girl was so close; there was no way he could lose. The thought of being able to play with both her and Laura filled Sam's head as he readily agreed.

'Good.' Laura undid his hands and told him to stand and take off his combats, which he did with great speed, his dick sticking out of the top of his boxers, its tip glistening.

Turning the volume up on the webcam, the room was flooded with the sounds of Jess's struggle to manage her breathing and delay her climax.

Sam had to concede that ensuring he could hear the girl's pleasurable torment was a clever move, as it added to his own growing desire.

Slipping off her dress, Laura turned the artist so she could see the screen while he buried his face between her breasts. As he feasted on her, Laura slipped her hand inside his boxers and wrapping her palm around his length, placed her thumb over his tip, and slowly caressed his cock.

Sam moaned softly into her flesh, trying his best to block out the sound of Jess in the background, who thanks to Miss Sarah's commanding voice, he knew to be on her hands and knees awaiting the next stage of her instruction.

'As you are busy and cannot see the screen, perhaps I should give you a running commentary, I'd hate you to miss anything.' Laura kept her voice level, not betraying how quickly Sam had enflamed her own body as he worked his tongue across her tits, his hands finding her hips.

The artist wanted to tell her not to, as it would only decrease his chances of winning, but he also felt a morbid curiosity to know what was happening. The images in his head couldn't have been any more lurid than those on the screen anyway.

'Miss Sanders is on the floor on all fours, and I can see the string of the love balls hanging from her pussy. Her arms are shaking with the effort of supporting herself, and her chest is swaying as it hangs down. There is something about that girl's breasts, don't you think? They simply scream to be smacked and then kissed better…'

Sam murmured into her flesh, trying to ignore the intense sensations swimming towards his groin.

'… Miss Sarah obviously enjoys them as well, for she has instructed the girl to stay immobile while she crawls beneath her. It looks as though Miss Sarah has decided she wants some fun of her own, she's taking her top off …'

Squeezing his eyes shut, Sam struggled not to turn and look at the screen. The pressure on his cock remained steady, and he could feel the need to come rising in the pit of his stomach.

'… Miss Sarah is naked. I knew from the moment I saw her six months ago that she was a woman who'd be a boon to the fifth floor. If anything, she's even more beautiful these days than she was then. She's lying beneath Miss Sanders and…' For the first time Laura faltered, her own body's craving for an orgasm flashing through her as Sam's hands slid to her clit. Taking a calming breath, she continued, '… Her lips have attached themselves to Jess's right tit, and a hand has snaked itself between her legs. Jess is close, I can see her trying to stay motionless, but her hips are rocking, and if you listen hard, Sam, you'll be able to hear her panting.'

Sam tried not to listen, but he couldn't help it. He needed to hear, needed to know that Jess was going to crack before he did.

'… Miss Sarah has swapped her mouth to the other tit, but is keeping up the attention on the right one with her hands. I confess I'm impressed. With the love balls in place I would have expected Jess to have come by now. I bet she's clenching her channel like mad so they don't fall out. They're probably slipping around inside her. You can tell by looking at the sheen on the top of her legs, that she's incredibly wet …'

Searching desperately for a way of both distracting Laura and breaking the tension that consumed his body, Sam said, 'Do you realise that when you're turned on, you stop calling your clerk by her surname, and start calling her Jess?' Then he bit Laura's nipple hard, making her yelp and break off her commentary. He'd hoped it would

143

make her cross, and deflect the steady rhythm of the hand on his cock. Instead Laura swiftly digested his observation of her possible weakness, before his hand raked across her body, allowing herself a moment's physical gratification, and a purr of arousal escaped her lips.

It was the purr that was Sam's undoing. He'd withstood days of waiting for her to call, being tied, taunted, and forced to watch live eroticism, but the combination of Laura's hand, and the sound of her arousal was too much for him. Against the background of Jess's heavy laboured breathing and Laura's sighs, Sam shot his load into Laura's busy fist.

'Oh I am sorry, Sam.' Mrs Peters did not sound sorry at all. 'You lost.' She physically twisted his face back to the computer screen. 'Jess is about to climax. Watch.'

He observed as Miss Sarah shuffled so that she was laying full length under the clerk, then, as Jess's moans turned to pleas, she yanked out the love balls, and stuck her mouth over the girl's sopping pussy. With a cry of release, Jess shuddered against the tongue, her arms shaking so much that she collapsed onto her tormentor, who quickly ordered her to lick her in return.

'The perfect 69. I'm going to have to keep an eye on those two. They seem to be getting on rather better than is professionally advisable.' Laura spoke thoughtfully, tapping off the screen, 'You lost, Samuel Wheeler, while Miss Sanders grows in her abilities every day. Maybe it's because she has accepted her submissive status, even if she won't say so out loud. Something you need to learn to do.'

'I am not going to be one of your toys, Laura.'

'Aren't you?' The manageress cocked her head on one side. 'We'll see.'

Sam felt a shiver run through his frame as she studied him. 'We will discuss that later. It will all depend on how you perform tonight, whether I decide if you should be shared or just kept for my own personal use.'

'You make me sound like a walking vibrator.'

Ignoring his attempt at humour Laura said, 'This evening I need you to do two things for me; the second concerns your help in Miss Sanders' continued training, the first ...' the manageress lay on the bed behind them, dragging him down on top of her, '... is obvious.'

Chapter Fourteen

THE ROOM WAS IN darkness when Lee ushered Jess inside. No lights or candles were lit, and the plush floor to ceiling velvet curtains were drawn.

There was no sign of life. Miss Sarah, Mrs Peters and her mysterious guest were not in evidence as the clerk and barman stood, a subdued erotic uncertainly sparking between them.

Jess glanced around the dim light of the Victorian study. It seemed an age since she'd visited the room to witness Master Philip receive his longed for punishment from Miss Sarah. Another life ago almost. A life where Jess had never even considered S&M, sex with women, or indeed sex with anyone at all for the most part, having settled for a happy life alone with a decent vibrator for company. Now, as her heart thudded in her ears, that quiet life seemed a foreign concept. There could be no going back.

A faint rustle from the corner of the room alerted Lee and Jess to the fact that they weren't necessarily alone after all.

Pointing in unison to the bottle green curtains, they watched the heavy fabric waft a fraction. There was no breeze in the room, no air conditioning, and the evening was too cold and damp for the windows behind the curtains to have been opened. There had to be someone there.

Jess and Lee exchanged glances. Were they allowed to look, or should they stay where they were, propped against the old desk in the centre of the room? The barman frowned as he whispered, 'We were told to stay here.'

'But did Mrs Peters mean stay exactly here against the desk, or here, within the room?' The curtains' movement was more obvious now, as if a foot was rhythmically kicking at them from the other side.

Not wanting to be the one who made the wrong decision, Lee hissed out his words, his eyes darting around the room, reminding Jess that they were probably being filmed, 'It's a test.'

Equally careful to remain unheard, Jess asked, 'But which sort of test? A test to see if we ignore whoever is behind there? Or a test to see what we do once we've found them?' Cold shivers ran down Jess's spine. She didn't like the fact of the unknown figure behind the curtains. *Can they hear everything we say? It has to be a person – doesn't it?*

'God knows.' Lee glanced at the wall clock, whose tick seemed to be getting louder as the minutes stretched by. 'It's your choice, not mine.'

'Why?'

'Because this is part of your education, your training. Not mine.'

'What?' Jess's mouth opened to ask what he meant, but closed hastily when she saw the warning expression on the barman's face. She may have been confused about many things concerning her place at Fables, but as she'd proved to Mrs Peters in the dungeon, Jess caught on quickly when it came to knowing when to stay quiet.

The curtain was swaying faster now, and as they

strained to listen, faint muffled sounds escaped from behind the velvet screen. Jess stepped forwards, almost on tip-toe, convinced she'd find a person behind the curtains. She wasn't sure who it would be, or in what state she'd find them. Her palms clammy, Jess took hold of both drapes and yanked them open.

On the wide hard wooden seat that formed the windowsill, bound, gagged, blindfolded, and with a pair of heavy duty headphones blocking out all sound, his legs fastened together at the ankles with a length of rope, sat a naked man. His impaired senses were straining, and tension oozed from every pore of his toned skin. Mumbled groans escaped from the corner of his ball-gagged mouth, while his outstretched arms, tied at the wrist to two hooks conveniently screwed into the walls either side of the window, rippled with fatigue.

'Who is he?' Jess was barely audible as she turned anxiously towards Lee, whose eyes were glued to the prisoner's stiff cock. 'Lee?' Jess placed her arm on the barman's sleeve, making him jump as if he'd been scalded.

'Mr Wheeler.'

'Mr Wheeler?'

'Mrs Peters' friend. She really likes him.'

Jess turned even paler than she was already as she regarded the incapacitated man. 'Likes him? Look what she's done to him.'

'I was sent to London to fetch him this morning. She must think he's really special.'

Whispering, Jess replied, 'Special in what way? I mean she's made him blind, deaf, and totally immobile!'

Lee simply smiled ruefully and very quietly said, 'Be careful Jess. Be very careful.'

The queue of questions lining up in Jess's throat was

halted before they could escape, as the door to the study was flung open. Jumping with a feeling of guilt she didn't understand, Jess watched as her boss strode into the room.

Laura Peters' voice cut through the atmosphere like ice, 'I believe I told you two to dress more appropriately.'

As one, Jess and Lee looked at their clothes. As neither of them lived in the hotel, they hadn't got clothes to change into, and their instructions to be at the study for 6.45 p.m. hadn't given them time to go home, change, and return. Jess had spent a frantic few minutes in the Ladies cloakroom splashing her face and wrists with cold water in an attempt to keep calm, adjusting her hold ups so they were at least level, and brushing lint off her black suit skirt and jacket.

Lee, whose tie was straighter than usual, with charcoal trousers devoid of their usual powdering of dust from the bar cellar, had obviously not had time to do much about his apparel either.

In contrast, Mrs Peters was wrapped in a magnificent hooded, ankle length velvet cloak in deep maroon, which showed nothing but the very bottom of the heeled black boots she wore. Jess was willing to bet that she wore something luxurious and incredibly sexy underneath, and was surprised at how much she wanted to see what it was like.

Miss Sarah, who had entered the study in Mrs Peters wake, waited without any sign of impatience by the closed door, resplendent in her Victorian study costume.

Mrs Peters, disapproval etched across her face, walked towards her prisoner. 'As Master Philips will have told you, Miss Sanders, our guest here is Mr Samuel Wheeler, a friend of mine. However, as you will have gathered from his restrained situation, he has a few issues with his position in our relationship.'

Jess swallowed carefully, trying not to let the surprise she felt that Mrs Peters even had a relationship, show on her face.

'Master Philips.'

Lee stood to attention, his hands clasped behind his back. 'Yes, Mrs Peters?'

'Your assistance will be required in maintaining our guests' helplessness during the evening.'

'Yes, Mrs Peters.'

Sensing Lee's growing excitement, Jess wasn't at all surprised when, on being commanded to remove his clothes, he revealed an already solid cock, which pointed greedily at the bound man.

'Ready for action as ever, Lee,' Miss Sarah slipped a short cane from its hiding place up her sleeve, running it suggestively between her fingers, a timely reminder to Lee of his lowly position in the order of things.

An approving half smile at the corner of Mrs Peters' lips was directed at her assistant, before she returned to the matter in hand. 'Miss Sanders, let me talk you through the situation we have here.' Walking to the chaise longue she sat down, and indicated Jess should join her. Unsure what to do with her hands, Jess squeezed them together on her lap, trying not to fidget. 'Miss Sarah is going to remove the headphones and ear plugs from our guest. It only seems fair that he hears what I'm about to say, although he can't see who I'm talking to, and his opportunity to put his side of things across will, of course, have to wait.'

With morbid fascination, Jess watched Miss Sarah take away the headphones. Mr Wheeler shook his head from side to side, and Jess could easily imagine how much he wanted to rub his ears after they'd been blocked for so long, but his tethered hands could do no more that rattle impotently against the hooks.

Jess found she was holding her breath as Mrs Peters' voice rose, her tone as sweet as syrup. 'Good evening, Sam. It is 7 p.m. now, so you've been in here for half an hour. As you will gather from the atmosphere and the muted shuffling around me, I have been joined in this beautiful study by three of my colleagues.'

A moment of disquiet trickled down Jess's spine to find herself described as a colleague, but she didn't have time to dwell on its significance as Mrs Peters was still talking. 'Miss Sarah, my right hand on the fifth floor is here, cane in hand as ever, along with Master Lee Philips, who you met earlier, along with Miss Sanders.

'Now, please bear with me a minute, Sam, I need to talk to Master Philips.' Turning to the barman, Mrs Peters was immediately more businesslike. 'I suspect it is a while since you had your cock sucked, Lee. That service will also be granted to you tonight. In the meantime please wait by the door. You will not need to be reminded, I'm sure, that you may not pleasure yourself in the meantime.'

Catching a glimpse of Lee's frustrated but accepting expression, Jess glanced back at the captive, who was agitating his chained hands and shaking his head for all he was worth. No one was being left in any doubt about how he felt towards the prospect of being sucked off by the younger man.

'Sam honestly,' Mrs Peters sounded like a teacher admonishing a wearing child, 'you'll love it when we get going. Now do be quiet, I need to explain things to Miss Sanders here. You remember Miss Sanders, Sam? She was the one we watched doing her exercises on the webcam earlier.'

Cold sweat prickled Jess's neck, and she turned to look

directly at Mrs Peters, before common sense took over and she dipped her gaze to the floor.

'Again you show me you are learning, Miss Sanders.' Mrs Peters' firm hand came to Jess's right leg, and the clerk felt her pulse accelerate as the palm began to glide up her leg, and under her skirt, until it reached the lacy top of her hold-up, where it waited, unmoving.

'Mr Wheeler here is considering a partial change of career. He is an artist, a very good one, but has been wasting his time and talent designing office blocks when he should be painting portraits.'

The tethered man stopped moving, listening intently to every sound in the room. Between the top of his blindfold and his hair line, Jess could see the deepening furrow of his brow.

'I invited him here today to discuss the possibility of coming to work with us on a part-time basis. I'm often asked to provide a mature male for our guests, and someone who can be both dominant and subservient would be perfect. As you will have guessed, Miss Sanders, it is his submissive side that needs the most work.'

Biting her lips together Jess concentrated hard on what her superior was saying, as well as fighting the temptation to squirm against the growing pressure on her leg that was inflaming her body as much as the strange situation around her.

'Sam and I have already proved to ourselves how sexually compatible we are, but he hasn't quite grasped the idea that I would be his boss. I'm not sure he has ever learnt to be much of a team player.'

Abruptly Mrs Peters stopped talking, her gleaming eyes glued to the prisoner. An expectant hush filled the room. The ticking of the clock on the wall seemed louder than ever. Jess felt like an actress in a play. All the characters were in place on the stage, and they were just waiting for Mrs Peters to direct them. Jess scanned the room. Mr Wheeler was very still now, obviously doing his best to relax despite his situation, Lee was propped against the wall, his lean body taut and erect, and Miss Sarah was sitting on the desk stool, her back straight, her fingers idly stroking her cane. Then there was Mrs Peters, resplendent in her robe, her bare crossed legs peeking through the folds as she sat next to Jess, her fingers still playing around the tops of her stockings.

Just as Jess became desperate to break the silence, Mrs Peters removed her hand and stood up. Taking up a position in the very centre of the room she addressed them all. 'As I have already informed Miss Sanders, the outcome of this evening will determine if she gets to stay on the fifth floor.' The manageress looked directly at Jess. 'You will need to impress me. If you don't, if you fail to throw off the last few reservations you have about the life we lead here, then you will be replaced, not just here, but downstairs as well.'

Jess's stomach churned. She felt both sick and excited as she listened, her pussy twitching in expectation.

'Master Philips and Miss Sarah here have both survived similar experiences. Many others have not.'

Chewing her bottom lip, Jess's eyes darted from Miss Sarah to Lee. They had known something like this would happen, but neither had said anything. Yet she still wasn't sure what "this" was, and how it could be her test when Mr Wheeler was the one so obviously incarcerated.

'Mr Wheeler is learning a lesson of his own.' Mrs Peters seemed to be reading Jess's mind again. 'The test, however, is yours. If you pass this, you'll face one final challenge … if not, well, I'm happy to recommend you to another hotel as a clerk. In that area, at least, you are capable.'

Her boss's compliment had all the barbs of an insult, and Jess was determined to pass this test, whatever it was. Now she'd accepted the fact that she couldn't go back to life alone with a vibrator, she wasn't even sure a regular boyfriend would be enough any more.

Jess's new acceptance of her situation however, didn't make her any more confident when it came to being face to face with three other more experienced people, all of whom were watching her intently, and would be totally indifferent to her failure.

'Miss Sarah, could you assist me please?' Mrs Peters stretched out a hand, into which her assistant immediately placed her cane, before standing respectfully behind her superior's shoulders awaiting instructions.

'Miss Sanders, I would like you to fetch the stool from the desk, and place it directly in front of Mr Wheeler.'

Jess found her hands shaking as she lifted the wooden seat and placed it before the captive.

'Now, I'd like you to remove his blindfold.'

Again Jess obeyed, taking care to be gentle as the tethered man was granted his sight. As he acclimatised himself to the subdued lighting, she stared into his blinking eyes trying to gain his sympathy, but instead she saw rage, and a deep hot lust which both fired her own desires and chilled her to the bone.

Mrs Peters laughed. 'If you're looking to Mr Wheeler for understanding Miss Sanders, then I fear you are looking in the wrong place. The poor man has been kept on the edge of climax for almost three hours now, and I don't think he'll have the energy or patience to concentrate on anything but getting what his body so badly needs.'

Sam tried to talk, but his gag smothered his words and a spray of frustrated spittle shot from the corners of his mouth.

'Once Sam tells me what I want to hear, then he'll be free to join in.' As she spoke, Laura Peters began to pace the study. 'Until that time, he will remain imprisoned.'

Jess wondered how he was supposed to make his intentions known when he was muffled, but was sensible enough not to ask. She was also afraid. She'd been frightened and nervous almost every moment since she'd been thrown out of her depth at Fables, but this was different. Jess had no doubt why she'd been asked to place the stool there, and she knew it was going to hurt. She wasn't sure she could withstand the show they were all about to put on, with her in the victim role, simply so Mr Wheeler would be turned on to the point that he'd give in to whatever demands Mrs Peters made of him.

'Undress, Miss Sanders.'

Peeling off her blouse and skirt, Jess was suddenly grateful for all the exhausting workouts she'd endured, which had given her more body confidence than she'd ever had. As she bent to roll down her hold ups, she accidentally caught Miss Sarah's eye. Although the other woman was conducting herself with the utmost professionalism, just for a second Jess could have sworn she saw a flash of something that seemed to resemble private desire. It was the same look she'd seen in her eyes early that morning when they'd licked each other out. The memory of that encounter sent extra zips of arousal coursing through her body, along with a sudden panic that Mrs Peters had seen it too. If she had, would she add to her punishment? Would Miss Sarah be chastised for it too?

Standing in only her bra and knickers now, Mrs Peters

spoke to Jess again, 'I've changed my mind. Remove those knickers, but keep your bra on. I think our guest should wait before he's rewarded with the sight of your chest, and Miss Sarah has probably seen enough of it for one day.'

Jess didn't dare glance at Miss Sarah to gauge her response to that comment, and did as she was told before standing with her hands behind her back.

'Over the stool please, Miss Sanders. Your hands can grip the legs one side, and your toes should just reach the floor on the other.'

Her heart thumped harder than ever, and her mouth dry. Jess positioned her tensed body over the wide wooden stool exactly as she'd been instructed, and waited.

Chapter Fifteen

WITH HER STOMACH SQUASHED against the stool and her hair hanging down the sides of her face, Jess really wished that Mrs Peters would just get on with it. Instead of being instantly spanked, however, to her surprise Jess found she had company as a naked Miss Sarah was directed to place a second stool before Mr Wheeler.

The fact Miss Sarah hesitated, even if only for a fraction of a second, as she leant over the seat was enough to tell Jess that she had not expected to be on the receiving end of her own cane.

If Miss Sarah hadn't understood why she was to be punished, Mrs Peters was only too delighted to inform her. From her copious velvet pockets she produced a small device. Crouching between the two prone women, she held it in the flat of her hand.

'A Dictaphone. As you know, there are many of these dotted about the Fables. Often they are accompanied by hidden webcams, but not always. Sometimes I ask Master Philips to place a portable bug in certain places for temporary use, such as in the gym …'

Jess lifted her head as Mrs Peters' voice trailed off meaningfully, and she realised that their boss must have overheard the conversation during her first exercise session. The manageress pressed a button on the small machine and Miss Sarah's words echoed around the study, "Personally I think Mrs Peters is wrong. No need to look so shocked that I'm admitting that. I happen to know that this room is not bugged, so I can do and say what I like. I'm also confident that you are not foolish enough to share my thoughts on this."

Miss Sarah said nothing as the Dictaphone was pointedly clicked off, but her chestnut hair swayed a little around her lowered head as she listened to the further charges laid against her.

'Then there was the little matter of the additional reward you gave to Miss Sanders after introducing her to Madam in the medical bay.'

This time Miss Sarah did protest, 'But that was a penalty! I was testing her. I wanted to know what was so damn special about the girl.'

'The fact remains that when you found out what that special quality was, rather than simply nurture it for our guests, you decided to enjoy it for yourself. As if that wasn't enough, there were the licked-tit rewards for sit-ups, the lack of an effective punishment to Miss Sanders for climaxing during exercise routines, and then of course, your merging of this morning's exercises into a 69 session.'

'But they were incentives! Something to keep her going, build up her stamina. Just like you used to for me!'

A tense hush descended on the already strained room. Mrs Peters' expression spoke volumes, but rather than venting her displeasure at Miss Sarah for sharing such information, the manageress merely continued with what she was saying, albeit through clenched teeth.

'Mr Wheeler and I have studied the tape. In fact Mr Wheeler enjoyed it so much he watched it twice while I was busy preparing him to witness this evenings test; a test which both you and Miss Sanders have to pass if you wish to stay here.'

'I'm good at my job, you've said so!' Shock, and the fear of losing a position she loved, made Miss Sarah bluster for a moment before she forced at least the appearance of composure on her face.

Continuing, Mrs Peters conceded, 'You are good at your job, and I would rather keep you than lose you, but I'm in charge here, and lately you seem to have forgotten that fact. I am supposed to be consulted before any of you indulge in any personal satisfaction. A rule you know very well, and one you have never broken until the temptation of Miss Sanders' presence was granted to us a few weeks ago.'

Jess couldn't believe what she was hearing. *Miss Sarah is being punished because of me!* Shuffling on the wooden stool, the wait to be spanked was overtaken by the wait to see how Miss Sarah would respond. Thinking back to her exercises that morning, Jess realised how it must have appeared on the webcam. She'd been so wrapped up in how fantastic going down on a woman felt while they were returning the favour that she hadn't thought beyond the moment. Now, time to think had been thrust upon her, Jess had to admit that when she'd seen Miss Sarah walk into the study, something in her had stirred; a hope that she would be the one to administer her correction, for if she did, she might well sweeten the penalty with a reward.

Brought out of her musings, by the sound of approaching footsteps, Jess turned her neck awkwardly and saw that Lee had hastened next to Mrs Peters'- side, a long leather lace in his hands.

'In order to make this impromptu competition fair, Miss Sanders' arms will be tied to the stool so she does not struggle or attempt to knock the cane away. You, Miss

Sarah, should not need the assistance of any type of restraint to keep you in place, for you have six months of experience and, as you say, you are very good at your job.'

The clerk didn't dare speak as Lee, his dick swinging dangerously in front of him, knelt and secured her wrists to the front legs of the stool with each end of the single lace. The barman tugged the leather so it bit into her skin, but then, at the last minute, with the briefest of conspiratorial nods, he loosened it a little, leaving Jess unaccountably grateful for this brief show of consideration, before he returned to his station by the door.

Keeping her head still, but glancing out of the corner of her eye, Jess could see Miss Sarah's knuckles, pale and stiff as they gripped the stool, and wondered if the dominatrix was regretting their additional activity that morning.

Leaving the two women for a moment, Mrs Peters placed a hand on either side of his face, bent forward and kissed Mr Wheeler's forehead. 'I hope you're enjoying the show, my dear.'

Sam nodded, knowing denial would have been ridiculous, as his encased dick strained against its leather holster. Despite his own predicament he was fascinated by this unexpected development. For it had been the two women now supplicated before him that had so distracted and captivated him on the small screen with their mutual oral sex, that Sam hadn't resisted Laura as she tied his arms to the hooks on the wall.

'I knew you'd appreciate seeing them naked again, Sam. I think I can promise you that the noises they make this time, however, will be less rapturous than before.' Mrs Peters undid his gag and kissed Sam full on the mouth, before leaving him gasping for air. Running his tongue over his lips in an attempt to moisten them, he opened his mouth to speak, but Laura placed a finger over his lips. 'Shush now, sweetheart. You may only speak when you are willing to say what I wish to hear.'

Mrs Peters glided majestically between the crouched women, trailing a single finger along each spine, making their skin visibly quiver beneath her touch. This tenderness, however, was short-lived, for seconds later Jess's arse was burning from the first strike of Miss Sarah's black cane, her strangled scream ricocheting off the walls.

Her own yell dying down, the clerk could hear the air echo around the cane again as Mrs Peters brought it down on Miss Sarah's buttocks with a resounding thwack, but only a small whistle of discomfort escaped from the other woman's gritted teeth.

As a second hit sent its blossom of pain through Jess's backside and straight to her breasts, where her nipples were grazing tantalisingly against her satin bra, her efforts to remain quiet failed. A loud hissed grunt shot from her mouth and her body rocked forward. Miss Sarah was still managing to maintain a still hush, and Jess realised that if she didn't concentrate harder on deflecting the effect of the increasingly fast strikes, then she'd have lost this competition, before it had begun.

Grateful her hands were tethered, forcing her to stay in place, Jess wondered again at the depth of Miss Sarah's self-discipline. She could easily knock the cane away, stand up and walk out. No one was forcing her to stay, yet here she stayed as Mrs Peters built up a criss-cross of pink strips across both her arse cheeks.

On the eighth stroke the tears that had been streaming down Jess's face were joined by sobs, even though she'd just begun to feel the warm glow of desire blossom from the blows, she'd abandoned her attempts to be silent. Miss Sarah, however, had turned her laboured breathing into a controlled sigh, and Jess realised that she was enjoying the sting.

Mrs Peters also noticed the subtle alteration to her assistant's reactions, and keen to deny her any further pleasure, immediately pocketed the cane. 'Round One to Miss Sarah.'

Jess groaned, her heartbeat hammering in time to her throbbing backside. Before she could recover, she felt Lee's hands back on her wrists. Untied, she was roughly manoeuvred so she sat on the stool, her sore arse smarting against the wood. Miss Sarah was also instructed to move, and Jess caught sight of her beautiful round butt, all lined and bruised with blotches of red, and felt an undeniable urge to kiss and lick it better.

Positioned face to face this time, Jess wasn't sure if she should catch the other woman's eyes in sympathetic understanding. *How much rivalry is there here anyway? We aren't up against each other are we? Surely we can both pass this test? Not really?* Her thoughts were interrupted by Lee's fingers fumbling with her bra strap. The freeing of her chest caused her to groan with relief in time to Mr Wheeler's whine of appreciation and, if her eyes weren't deceiving her, the further dilation of Miss Sarah's pupils.

'Round Two.' Mrs Peters walked to the desk, and began to search through its drawers. 'You will put your hands on your heads, where they will stay while Lee and I attend to your chests. The loser will be the one to move first. I assume I don't need to tell you that you are not permitted to come.'

Gesturing to the barman to attend, Mrs Peters gathered

together two quill pens. Jess felt her stomach recoil. She could already imagine what it would be like to feel the plush feather from one of the quills run over her breasts, and wasn't sure how long she'd be able to hold off the orgasm she was sure they'd engender. Again, Jess flicked her eyes up at Miss Sarah. Her head was erect on her shoulders, her back was straight, and infuriatingly her hands were placed casually on her head rather than clasped together like Jess's.

Lee placed a small wooden table between the women and the watching Mr Wheeler. Then Mrs Peters arranged a small pot of black ink and some blotting paper on the table and passed a quill to Lee, who stood before Miss Sarah.

'Remember, ladies, you will not move an inch.'

Drawing in a sharp breath, Jess watched Mrs Peters and Lee dip the pointed ends of the quills into their inkwell, tap them onto the blotting paper, and then approach.

She'd been so sure she was about to be tickled with the feather, that the sharp, yet intensely sensual feel of the quill nib as it trailed ink across the top of her right breast was totally unexpected. Miss Sarah's expression showed that she was equally surprised by the brand of torture that was being employed, and her angry green eyes shone with a deep glaze of lust and determination.

Prevented from looking down by the instruction not to move, Jess tried to read what Lee was writing across Miss Sarah's flesh, as her own skin was caressed and scratched by the loops and flourishes of Mrs Peters' handwriting. Every few seconds the protagonists would fill the quills with fresh ink, Jess became almost hypnotised watching Lee add ink, write his deepest darkest desires across the luscious tits of his mistress, and then refill his quill again.

Jess wondered what Mrs Peters was writing. Each stroke of ink sent flutters of need from her chest to her crotch. Her right breast had been covered, and her boss was already working her way across the second, making sure that the clerk knew when she'd finished a sentence with a brutally sharp full stop.

Her arms were beginning to ache, and the hair trapped beneath Jess's palms felt sticky. Closing her eyes, she tried to banish the picture of Miss Sarah's tits, covered in requests from Lee to be sucked off, buggered, and generally seen to in a vast number of ways. She opened them again almost immediately, however, as the sensations the quill sent zipping through her increased ten-fold in the darkness of her own imagination. The clerk could feel the juice, that had been building up since she'd arrived in the study, leak from her pussy, trickle down her thighs, and dot the wooden seat. With every swipe of the nib, an additional ripple of need hit Jess's nervous system. The desire to move, to stretch her arms, to shuffle her bruised backside, and to look down at what had been temporary tattooed on her was becoming extreme. *When would they stop? Would they keep going until one of them moved?* Jess knew she couldn't afford to lose this game.

Abruptly, Mrs Peters signalled to Lee, and they both rested their quill pens back into the inkwell. Simultaneously, the women let out suppressed ragged noises of relief, both confused as to why the writing had stopped before either of them had failed the test.

'I'm impressed ladies.' Mrs Peters nodded. 'Stage Two I think, Master Philips.'

What the hell will they do next? Jess watched as both quills were filled with ink, before both nibs were placed on the very tip of each woman's right nipple, and squeezed.

The gasp that shot from Miss Sarah's lips as a cascade of cold black ink ran down her ultra receptive teat was drowned out by the startled yelp from Jess as she experienced the same sensation. As excess ink dribbled down the ladies' creamy flesh, Mrs Peters and Lee picked up a small square of blotting paper each, and begun to rub them over the inked tits. Instantly Jess felt her body go into overdrive as the rough paper scrubbed at her inflamed breasts. Biting her tongue hard to deflect her orgasm Jess felt blood drip down her throat as the delicious torture continued.

Now the women did look at each other and Jess felt Miss Sarah's cat-like eyes lock with hers, but Jess wasn't sure if she was willing her to hang on, or willing her to fail. As more squares of blotting paper were placed across their hot inky skin, much of the dribbled ink merged with the previously written sentences, into a spidery mass of black lines and swirls.

Jess could feel her pussy contract as Mrs Peters kept up the buffing of her right nipple, while smoothing a piece of blotting paper down between her legs, pulling it away the second it brushed the her clit. Jess whimpered out loud, as her boss held the paper up to Mr Wheeler. 'Look at this, Sam, our naughty little clerk is so wet!

Mr Wheeler's lips were almost white from being clamped shut in his desperation not to make a sound and this incur further punishment on himself. His eyes were relentlessly watching, soaking up every detail of the action before him. Jess saw, as she struggled to control her own pulse-rate, that the artist's dick had begun to leak precome around the edge of his cock-case.

'Master Philips, blot Miss Sarah please.'

Lee obeyed, pushing a piece of the green paper between the mistress's legs, before holding it up for inspection.

'Wet, very wet. In fact, if we compare papers, then I would say that Miss Sarah may well be wetter than Miss Sanders. So this round goes to the clerk.' Mrs Peters paused, her gaze briefly meeting the glare of her assistant who could see from a look at the paper, that the manageress's claims were patently untrue. 'It may well be that you have much better self-discipline, Miss Sarah, but in this game every aspect of bodily control must be considered.'

Jess could hardly believe what she was hearing. Surely there was no physical way you could control how wet you became. Suddenly she realised that it didn't actually matter who had really won the round, Mrs Peters was determined to take this competition, and both its unwilling contestants, right to the wire.

Chapter Sixteen

'FINAL ROUND,' MRS PETERS announced in her most imperious voice, 'Master Philips, I need you to assist me to move things round a little.' Lee nodded as Mrs Peters continued, 'Ladies, you may relax for a moment.'

Every inch of Jess longed to be touched and she realised just how clever Mrs Peters had been to bring such an abrupt halt to the last round, for she had been on the brink of coming and was convinced Miss Sarah couldn't be that far behind her.

The presence of Mr Wheeler wasn't helping Jess's situation. She saw the frustration in his eyes as he observed Mrs Peters lead Lee into the far corner of the room, and begin to whisper in his ear. The barman then, having nodded in agreement, knelt before Mr Wheeler and began to undo the cock case.

Sam let out a guttural sigh that might have been relief, or might have been in protest, as his shaft was freed, a sigh that morphed into a needy groan as the young man's fingers deftly played over his taut pink rod.

Mrs Peters studied her lover with critical fascination as the barman continued to massage his cock. Then, her cloak billowing around her, she unlocked Mr Wheeler's arms, instructed Lee to sit on the window seat next to him, and crisply ordered Miss Sanders and Miss Sarah to kneel before them both.

Stationing herself between her crouched workforce and the artist, Mrs Peters slid her gown to the floor. The heart-stopping thud as the velvet hit the carpet brought a further level of tension to the atmosphere of the Victorian Study. From her position of meek submission, Jess couldn't see her boss beyond her heeled and laced boots, but could tell from the audible moan of appreciation that escaped Mr Wheeler, that Mrs Peters looked as magnificent as ever.

'Round Three, the decider if you like, is based on technique as well as stamina.' As she spoke, the manageress took the chains that had previously fastened Sam to the wall, and used them to tie the men's wrists behind their backs. Then she collected up Mr Wheeler's discarded blindfold, took another from the desk, and placed them securely over both of the men's eyes.

'Gentlemen, before you stand two beautiful women. One is a fairly naive born submissive, the other a natural dominatrix, who has seen and done more than you can possibly imagine. Yet they could each learn from each other.'

Jess could sense Miss Sarah bristling at this, and she wondered what on earth she could possibly teach her fellow contestant.

'Please stand, ladies.' Relieved they were allowed to stretch, both women took the chance to flex their limbs.

'Listen carefully, gentlemen. Shortly Miss Sarah and Miss Sanders will kneel before you, taking it in turns to give you a blow job. You will not be told who is attending to you. After two minutes of attention the women will swap places. Once you have experienced both mouths you must award each session a mark out of ten. The winner will stay an employee of the fifth floor. The loser will face a further challenge in Room 54. Then, if they succeed in that challenge, it will be decided if both women will be staying at Fables. Should the demand of Room 54 defeat them, then a new vacancy at Fables will be advertised in next week's paper.'

Already in a state of extreme anxiousness, Jess felt her chest tighten with the prospect of her certain defeat. She was woefully inexperienced at giving blow jobs, and could tell from the glint in Miss Sarah's eye that this was a game she was more than confident of winning.

'Edge forward and open your legs wider,' Mrs Peters addressed the blinded men. Then, taking both her female assistants by the hand, she led them before the men, and with a brief press to their shoulders, pushed Miss Sanders before Lee, and Miss Sarah down before Sam.

Jess wasn't sure if she was pleased to have the barman first, or if she'd wanted to get Mr Wheeler over with, as she was convinced he was more likely to come, considering the state he'd been kept in all evening.

'You may use you hands as well as your mouths. Should your appointed partner come, then it is you, not them, who will have lost. Your challenge is to keep them on the brink of satisfaction, but not to tip them over the edge.'

Her eyes glued to the dangerously rigid cock before her, Jess frantically tried to remember descriptions of blow jobs she'd read in the few erotic novels she kept at home. Doing her best to ignore the sheen of sweat prickling across her flesh, and her own body's lustful craving for a climax, Jess jumped with nervous energy as Mrs Peters called out, 'Begin!'

Seeing Miss Sarah dive eagerly to the new task, Jess gingerly enveloped Lee's sticky length and shut her eyes. Relaxing her throat as best she could, she inched forwards, placing a supporting hand beneath his balls, and was instantly rewarded with a mutter of satisfaction. This boosted Jess's confidence for a second, before panic that he was about to come took over, and she drew back. This sudden loss of sensation however, made Lee moan more, and his dick felt harder than ever.

Faint murmurs of approval were coming from Mr Wheeler, but Jess daren't open her eyes to see lest Miss Sarah's obvious expertise made her feel even more inferior.

The two minutes seemed to be taking a lifetime to pass as Jess dredged her memory to recall a particularly erotic scene from one of her kinky novels, and began to copy the actions of the fictional heroine by licking around the tip of Lee's dick while kneading its base and running a stray finger toward his anus. Again he moaned, but this time the clerk kept up the action, willing his tight cock not to spunk, as the seconds ticked slowly by, as the long forgotten story came back to her.

'Thirty seconds to go!'

Jess slowed her tongue and began to ease Lee's shaft deeper into her throat, but rather than pumping against it, she clamped her mouth tightly around him for a few seconds, and then released him briefly, before clamping him again. She could feel his enjoyment of this new move, and was just beginning to enjoy her unaccustomed level of control, when Mrs Peters announced, 'Time Up. Withdraw.'

Dropping the barman's dick, Jess risked a glance at his face, hoping she'd made some sort of impact, and would get a good score. The drawn out sigh Lee gave was certainly encouraging, but she felt less hopeful when she saw the smug expression on Miss Sarah's face. Jess knew without a doubt that Mr Wheeler had been taken right to the edge of climax, and had been left there. It wasn't going to take much to tip him over now it was her turn to attend to him.

'Swap.'

Retrieving as much saliva as she could from the back of her throat, Jess moistened her dehydrated mouth and reluctantly knelt before the artist. She would lose this contest. There was little question of that, but Jess was damn sure she'd make it last as long as she could. So she would at least go out fighting with some of her dented pride still intact.

'Begin.'

Again Jess closed her eyes, but rather than engulf the new shaft, she softly began to blow around its balls and up along the length. The dick twitched, and she could smell the saltiness of his precome, but not the instant explosion she'd feared, and the other two women had undoubtedly expected.

Determined to keep him aroused and gain a decent score, Jess pushed her right hand under his backside, and with an accommodating shuffle from Mr Wheeler, eased the very end of her index finger inside his anus, altering his groans to grunts, as opening her mouth wide, she finally took him within. Barely touching his length but for the lightest caress with her tongue and the briefest touch of the side of her throat, with an aching jaw, Jess subjected Mr Wheeler to a tantalisingly light pressure, while her breathing escaped in puffs from the corner of her lips.

Jess had been concentrating so hard, that she barely heard Mrs Peters' 30-second-warning, but her concentration was shattered when, from nowhere, a firm hand snaked between her legs and tapped her sodden pussy. Jess couldn't help but start against the intrusion, and in doing so, suddenly deep throated the artist, triggering climaxes in them both, as Mrs Peters' treacherous fingers found her clit and pinched it twice in quick succession.

As spunk shot down her throat, Mr Wheeler yelled out with long held back satisfaction, and Jess spasmed with joyous frustrated defeat. There was nothing she could do but let the orgasm rip through her comparatively untutored body.

When the clerk finally stopped shaking; the artist's come still trickling down her chin, she sat like a statue, waiting for the oncoming storm of outrage from Mrs Peters and gloating from Miss Sarah. She didn't want to look at any of the other people in the study, and an angry realisation dawned on her. She was willing to bet that Miss Sarah hadn't been interfered with, only her. Once again they had intended for her to fail from the start, and when it looked as if she might actually complete the challenge, Mrs Peters had interceded so she'd lose. For the first time, Jess began to wonder just how much of a set up this had all been. *Did Miss Sarah know she was going to be included in this session all along?*

Jess sagged with a feeling of hopeless exhaustion. *Well, they've got what they wanted.* Her stomach clenched into a sharp knot as she wondered what she would have to face next.

Chapter Seventeen

THEY'D ALLOWED HER A shower, a light meal, a large drink of water and three hours in one of the guest rooms to sleep. Jess hadn't slept though. Her body ached too much, her backside throbbed, and the spectre of what might await her behind the door of Room 54 had become more lurid and horrific by the minute. When the knock on the door that told Jess they were ready for her finally came, she was more relieved than frightened.

The room was white. Walls, ceiling, door and even the blinds pulled over the windows were white. A bare light bulb hung from a central white cable.

Jess had expected complicated instruments of correction, items of submission that would make the dungeon seem as if it was merely somewhere to play. She had mentally prepared herself for a scene from an extreme porn film. What she hadn't expected, was virtually nothing.

Only three items met Jess's gaze. First, in one corner of the room was the habitual camcorder. Secondly, a large white rimmed television, with no visible means of switching it either on or off, had been fastened in the centre of one wall. However, it was the third item that made her blood chill and dominated all her attention. A large white rope hammock had been strung across the room, attached by a pivot system to a sturdy white wooden frame.

She didn't waste her energy bothering to protest as Miss Sarah and Lee hoisted her naked body, face down, into the hammock. But Jess couldn't prevent her cry of alarm, as the rope net swung alarmingly. Her cries increased as Lee's fingers dragged her tits through two of the gaps in the wide rope weave. Crouched beneath the hammock he pulled at her tender flesh until both her breasts were poking through as far as it was possible for them to go.

Rough and prickly, the rope irritated Jess's captive chest as well as squeezing it into a strange shape. The tight band around the base of each globe dug savagely into her skin, while the remainder of her tits hung down, feeling oddly free by comparison, and yet immensely vulnerable.

Jess's face was pressed firmly against the hammock, the criss-cross of white rope chaffing her cheeks and chin as Miss Sarah manoeuvred her, forcing her jaw open so she had little choice but to bite into a section of the rope, as if she was a horse champing a bit. With her hair flopping down at the side of her face, Jess peered through the gaps in the hammock to the floor, her eyes watering at the sheer whiteness of it all.

There was no need to tie her feet and hands. Feeling she resembled a beached whale, Jess's only way of getting out of the hammock would be to rock hard enough so she fell out, and that would mean risking ripping her breasts from her body.

Wriggling in an attempt to become marginally more comfortable made the hammock swing again, and Jess, her heart pounding at every pulse point in her body, looped her fingers through the thick net, a squeal of alarm escaping from the corners of her mouth. Her terror seemed to amuse Miss Sarah as Lee grabbed her knees and wedged them firmly in between two of the gaps in the weave, securing her as firmly as if she'd been knotted into place.

Jess wondered if Lee or Miss Sarah had been allowed to come since their encounter in the study. They were both dressed again now, and Jess felt an irrational stab of jealousy to think they could have enjoyed each other without her. The thought made her sigh. Here she was, captured in a headache-inducing white room against a hideously uncomfortable rope bed, and yet she was envious of her tormentors. She knew once and for all there was no way she could leave the Fables now. *If only they'd tell me what I'm supposed to do.*

At last her mute companions finished getting her into position; face down, bosom trapped, legs apart. Miss Sarah knelt beneath Jess's head and stared up at her. 'I've been instructed to inform you that you will stay here until Mrs Peters considers you worthy, or not, of life on the fifth floor. A few people will come and go. Sometimes they'll have been given permission to let you come.

'This is the ultimate endurance test. It's all about stamina; the most important skill to have here, and in one way or another, we've all experienced the hammock.' Then Miss Sarah reached up and kissed Jess's cheek through the net and whispered so the camcorder couldn't hear, 'I was in on the last challenge, you were right in your suspicions. Such fun to watch the confusion on your face.'

Jess was abandoned then, the pressure from the ropes making her breasts ache and swell despite the gravitational pull. The quiet air they left behind them seemed to vibrate off the walls. Jess spat out the rope gag, but her attempts to look around her made the hammock quiver, and sent spasms of pain along every nerve in her chest, which she'd begun to worry might be permanently damaged if she moved too much. Jess could imagine her hidden audience laughing as they watched her via the webcam. Wishing it would stop swaying, she gripped harder, wrapping her fingers and toes deeper around and under the rope bed.

While tensing her body in her continuous attempts to remain motionless, the faintest of sounds filtered through Jess's consciousness. At first she couldn't work out where it was coming from, but as the gentle hum grew in volume, she realised that the television screen on the wall to her left had been activated.

Very carefully, Jess craned her neck to see what was on the screen, but the hammock shifted and fresh bursts of pain tore through her tits, and so she sank bank onto the bed, clamping the rope back between her teeth for extra safety.

The volume from the television's speakers continued to grow, and Jess's imagination was incapable of not going into overdrive as she heard her own voice. It was her and Lee in the school room. The barked orders of Mrs Peters filled Jess's ears as she recalled that day; stretched over the desk, tormented, tied and teased. Jess realised with an abrupt clarity, as she pictured Lee wielding the paintbrush over her flesh in time to the echo of her groans, that being been made to wait so long for her climax that day had been a valuable lesson to surviving life on the fifth floor.

Jess's breasts throbbed. She could feel them chaff and her nipples harden as her tired body was re-aroused to the reverberation of her own pleasure. On the screen Lee was bringing her to orgasm. Again, Jess felt compelled to see the television, but the metal cogs that supported the hammock against its frame squeaked perilously, and although it only rocked slightly, Jess's body clenched with fresh discomfort, and the fear of being tipped onto the unforgiving shiny white-tiled floor.

With the room resounding to her own sighs and moans, Jess's pussy felt slick in sympathy with her past desires. She wanted to block out the noise with her hands, but daren't let go of the ropes. She couldn't believe how badly her exhausted body wanted some fresh attention; any attention. *If only they'd start whatever they are going to do.* Echoes of her previous climaxes had died down on the television, and a few seconds of quiet soothed Jess for a moment, only to be replaced by the unmistakeable hum of a cane being arched through the air. Jess's body flinched in sympathy, and she clenched her arse cheeks in automatic response to the memory of the old assault.

When was it? Who's on the receiving end? Jess searched through her recent past, and suddenly recognised the muted cries of Master Paul, the very first guest she had encountered at Fables. That meant the whip hand belonged to Miss Sarah, and Jess's crotch spasmed in instant recognition of that fact. She could see her so clearly in her mind, their exercise sessions imprinted on her brain and body for ever. The stamina she'd been teaching Jess to develop was really coming into its own now.

Jess's thoughts froze as the door behind her opened, and unseen feet padded across the floor. *Male,* Jess thought, *male with bare feet, and turned on if the quality of his breathing is anything to go by.*

She didn't try and look at the visitor for fear of moving the hammock. Jess didn't think it was Lee, but supposed it might be Sam Wheeler, or maybe even a paying guest; one of Mrs Peters' regulars enticed by the chance to assist with her tutelage; Mr Proctor perhaps?

The footsteps stopped, and Jess thought the newcomer must have paused to watch the television. The gasps that were oozing from its speakers were a mixture of her own as Mrs Peters massaged her clit, and Master Paul's as Miss Sarah ordered him to attend to her chest.

The pause was short lived. Rough fingers pulled at her legs, widening them carelessly, making the hammock sway once more. Crying out in anguish for her breasts, Jess fought to relax her limbs to make their manoeuvring easier. At last, with knees bent outwards and forced through new holes, her feet hooked over the sides of the hammock, the calloused hands, which Jess was now convinced she'd not felt before, let her go and the footsteps disappeared from the room, the door shutting behind him.

She felt more precarious than ever as the television switched to the voice of Miss Sarah ordering her to do ten more sit ups. Instantly her mouth could taste the memory of the mistress's pleasingly rough areoles, and Jess had to swallow back the urge to scream for them to get on with whatever they were planning. The volume of the film increased again and Jess's own whines as her past self was ordered to ride the exercise bike while holding in love-balls became merged with her new tears, as the discomfort and frustration of her inaction began to wear her down.

She didn't hear the door to Room 54 being re-opened above the crescendo of noise coming from the speakers. Jess could do nothing to block out the sound of her on screen orgasm, and even less to remove the images that played in her head of all the mouth, lips, tongues and fingers that had traced their way over her body during the past month. Not to mention the whips, canes and countless other instruments of erotic and exotic instruction she'd so recently experienced.

When hands came to her pussy, Jess thought she was dreaming it at first, that they'd spilled over from the fantasy world that her short confinement in the white room had brought her. It was only when a hasty digit pushed its way through the rope weave and up inside her that Jess realised the sensation of being filled at last was actually real.

As the anonymous finger was joined by a hand, squeezing and kneading at Jess's cunt, scraping her clit until the knot of climax gathered in her stomach, Miss Sarah came and stood in front of her. Bleary eyed, the clerk tried to focus on the mistress, her brain registering that if she was standing there, then someone else was playing with her. Another female if the length of fingernails and texture of the skin was to be believed.

'Do you see what I have here, Miss Sanders?' Miss Sarah knelt beneath her, staring up into Jess's dull eyes, holding up a large plastic, clear, hollow dildo. It was thicker than any sex toy Jess had ever seen.

Blinking back her disbelief that anyone could accommodate such a tool, Jess's eyes strayed to the crouched woman's breasts, half hidden and half exposed by a deliciously tight-laced soft-brown leather basque.

She shouldn't have looked. The fingers between her legs had increased activity, pushing and pumping at her cunt, while a fingernail flicked relentlessly at her clit. Jess couldn't help it, and was too exhausted to battle her own feelings. With her eyes fixed on Miss Sarah, and the possibilities of what she and the two inch thick dildo she was holding might bring, Jess spasmed violently.

Miss Sarah shot a hand out to steady the hammock, which swung against the force of Jess's orgasm, as the unknown fingers slid away. Bathed in sweat, the final tremors of the clerk's climax trembled through the coarse rope against which she was trapped.

'Better?' Miss Sarah's voice was inescapably sarcastic, and Jess didn't answer. 'You need to be more careful, Miss Sanders. Your chest could easily have become damaged if I hadn't been here to hold you steady.' She stroked the end of each hanging globe with her palm. Jess cried out, the mix of pain and desire making fresh tears spring into her eyes.

'They are so red, right now.'

Another sound filtered into Jess's consciousness. Lee appeared in her eye line. He was naked now, and the hungry expression that he hid so well when he was on duty behind the bar was in full evidence. He held up a harness that Jess recognised as being of the same style as the chastity belt she'd worn before, although it lacked the sheepskin irritant. 'This is going to be threaded through the hammock's rope, and strapped around you. It will keep the dildo nicely in place.'

Disappearing beneath Jess, he pushed the strap through a hole in the hammock, tugging and pinching her flesh as he worked. When at last the leather belt was in place, Miss Sarah held the hollow plastic dildo back up in front of Jess's face before passing it to the barman.

Desperately trying not to tense up even more, Jess felt the thick tip against her opening. For a second she thought perhaps her senses had tricked her eyes into thinking it was wider that it really was. A moment later she knew her initial assessment had been correct. Despite being wet, uncertainty and fear had locked Jess's muscles, and as Lee jammed the clear shaft inside her, she let out a strangled whimper around the edges of the rope.

Taking no notice of her discomfort, Lee delighted in

spending an agonisingly protracted ten minutes easing the dildo in place, before securing it with the chastity belt.

Sore where the itchy hemp touched, stretched further open than she'd ever been before, and with breasts that felt as if they were both on fire and numb at the same time, Jess hardly dared breathe as without a word her companions left the room.

It was only after they'd gone that Jess attention returned to the television, and her torment was immediately increased by the reverberation of her own howling, as she was spanked in the school room. Flushing with renewed shame, she remembered how badly she'd needed to feel the sting that day. Her backside, the buckle from the belt digging in just above her vulnerable arse cheeks, tingled as the remembrance of each slap reverberated around the white walls.

An anxious lump formed in Jess's throat. With her torso trapped and her pussy jammed with the uncomfortably stout and yet frustratingly light dildo, she realised that the only thing left for her next visitor to abuse was her backside.

Scared that Mrs Peters would somehow read her mind again and think that was what she wanted, Jess tried to concentrate on something else, but it was impossible, and she wasn't at all surprised when the door to Room 54 re-opened and two palms unceremoniously slapped her arse, making her body judder and the dildo dance within her.

Half crying, half mewling, Jess felt herself reacting to the hands that swapped spanking for smoothing their way up and down her legs. Male hands Jess judged by their size, but they didn't feel like Lee's. She felt as if she was being polished, as the yells from the screen reached a tumultuous conclusion.

Her previous climax seemed a lifetime ago, but Jess

was convinced Mrs Peters wouldn't be impressed if she came again so soon. Managing to breathe steadily, despite all that had happened to her, Jess flinched as another slap met her right buttock, and the television was switched off.

A further smack landed on her left side. Jess's teeth bit hard into the rope, and she felt an odd ripple of pride as she successfully held in her cry of pain.

Everything sped up then. The smacks rained harder and faster, and the hammock swung perilously.

Suddenly, there was Mrs Peters, attired as carefully as ever in a stunning maroon basque and suspenders. She knelt beneath Jess with all the haughty dignity of an empress. 'You appear to be enjoying your training in Room 54.'

"Enjoying" wasn't the word Jess would have chosen. She concentrated on not whining as the beating continued, each stroke putting extra strain on her tits and pussy.

'I'm sure you have a lot going on in your mind at the moment, so I'll clarify the situation for you.' Mrs Peters lay full length on the floor beneath Jess so she didn't have to crick her neck to talk to her.

Jess watched her boss, so close, yet untouchable, knowing that her chest dangled just inches from potential stimulation.

'I do hope you've appreciated the background accompaniment I provided for you. Lee had a very happy hour putting that short film together. I honestly don't think I've ever seen him so stiff.'

Biting harder into the hammock, Jess could feel the rope begin to cut at the sides of her mouth as Mrs Peters critically assessed her. For a glorious split second Jess thought she was going to reach out and touch her, and she couldn't contain her sigh of disappointment when that didn't happen.

'You must curb that impatience, child.' The manageress put her hands to her own breasts, and Jess felt jealousy shoot from every fibre of her being as the older woman pleasured herself instead of her. 'Where was I? Oh yes, your chest is gorgeously restrained, I just adore the way it wobbles each time Mr Proctor (you remember him I'm sure), spanks your backside. A backside, I must say, that is decidedly trimmer than when you arrived with us five weeks ago. Miss Sarah must be congratulated on such an effective exercise routine, you are both fitter and yet not horribly thin. I'll never understand women who believe men like stick women. Anyway, I digress.

Most interestingly of all, however, is that dildo so firmly wedged inside you; I can appreciate how strange it must feel, Miss Sanders. Incredibly wide, pushing the walls of your channel to their capacity, and yet at the same time, it has no weight to it at all.'

Beads of sweat dribbled down Jess's breasts, a glistening drip hung from her left nipple. Jess willed it not to fall, but her willpower was not enough to defeat gravity.

As the moisture hit Mrs Peters flesh, she spoke coolly, 'It appears you are rather hot. Perhaps you'd like a nice wet tongue to lap at you for a while?'

Jess's fervent nod made Mrs Peters laugh. 'Now, two things are about to happen, and I think it's only fair to warn you about them.'

Every hair on Jess's body stood on end. If Mrs Peters felt she needed warning then it had to be something pretty extreme.

'The first is that you are to have some company in here; the second is that the hammock you are resting on is attached to its frame by a pivot system. It can therefore be made lower and higher at will. This is about to happen.'

A cold shiver engulfed Jess, and her fingers automatically gripped the sides of the hammock so tightly her skin began to whiten.

'You've had only one climax so far, I'm impressed. However, whether you stay here, employed on the fifth floor will depend on how long you can go without another one. If you can beat the time of your predecessor, before you grant your body the freedom to let go, then you'll be allowed to stay.'

Jess's voice was croaky, 'How long did she last?'

Mrs Peters merely smiled and shook her head. 'I'll tell you that afterwards.'

Jess had almost forgotten about the artist. His confinement in the study seemed an eternity ago. Yet, now Mr Wheeler was standing before her. Naked, his wrists bound in front of him, his solid penis sheathed, his body radiating desire.

Jess wondered if he'd caved in, if he'd finally agreed, once and for all, to be the slave the manageress wanted him to be, or if he'd been enduring further punishment of his own. He certainly looked as frantic for some relief as she felt.

'Into position please, Sam.' On Mrs Peters' words the artist lay down beneath Jess, in almost exactly the same position his lover had occupied only moments before.

With little choice but to peer into his eyes, Jess took in their greed as he stared, not at her face, but at her breasts. She wished he was able to touch them.

Tilting her chin as much as she dared, Jess flicked her gaze over Sam's body. His dick was sticking up like an incongruous flag pole.

'Thank you, Master Philips.' Mrs Peters signalled to Lee, who stood at the other end of the hammock, and suddenly Jess let out a gut wrenching squeal as it dropped. Her eyes streamed and her stomach flipped at her sudden drop, as the rope rocked and hot stabbing pains flared through her breasts.

Mr Wheeler had obviously been expecting the hammock to fall, but he couldn't contain a flinch as it came towards him. Jess could feel his breath on her face. This was a worse torture than anything that had gone before. Sparks of pure want surged between them, both wanting, both desperate.

With pussy-twitching frustration Jess waited, every second lasting for ever, making it impossible for her to judge how much time had gone by.

Miss Sarah and Lee remained at the head and foot of the hammock. No one spoke. No one moved. Her neck ached and her fingers and toes felt numb with the effort of gripping. Mr Wheeler was so close to her, but he might as well have been a million miles away. His eyes remained fixed on her tits, which glowed red after being trapped and hanging for so long.

The artist's hands fidgeted against his chest. He could so easily have lifted them up at the elbows and handled her. Jess could imagine how much determination he was employing to stop himself from doing just that.

Without warning, the hammock dropped another inch, and Jess's stomach lurched, and a lump of bile rose in her throat. The air danced between them as Jess yelled out in shock. Sam grunted at their frustrating closeness.

Jess could smell her companion now. Sweat mixed with the sticky scent of precome and heavy lust. Only one more inch and Mr Wheeler's dick would be brushing her skin, teasing its wet head against her mound. Jess tried and failed to stop thinking how good that would be, how amazing it would feel if the hammock dropped again, when her body would only be separated from the artist's by the ropes alone, her chest crushed against his, his cock pushing to get into her already full pussy. She closed her eyes. If she kept thinking like that she'd come before another finger was laid on her, which she suspected was Mrs Peters' intention.

Not bothering to disguise her heavy breathing, Jess panted hot air over the man below, wondering what would happen if he came before her.

As the seconds ticked by, Jess braced herself. *Surely the hammock will move again soon? How will I be able to stop myself climaxing? Sam's wearing a condom, so he must be expecting to fuck – but will it be me he screws?* Her exhaustion was forgotten; only the determination to succeed remained.

Sam raised his elbows a fraction and Jess's breath snagged in her throat as she thought some attention was about to be given to her tits, only for it to turn into a groan as he overcame his moment's weakness and returned his tethered arms to his chest.

Then Miss Sarah was standing next to them, a half smile playing at the corner of her mouth. Remaining quiet, she edged past, taking care not to touch them. Then, with her delicate fingers she undid the belt that kept the hollow dildo in place. Jess whimpered as the thick plastic was eased out of her, leaving her emptier and wider, than she'd ever been before.

A new urgency consumed Jess. She needed to be refilled. And she needed it now. Nothing else mattered. She could feel the liquid that had gathered around the plug smeared against her snatch and drip onto the prisoner below, whose own moans told Jess his desire to fuck her was growing out of all proportion now the way was clear for his cock.

Flames of agony coursed through her breasts as, finally, the hammock fell again There was now only a thin film of air between her and the artist. If she strained, she could probably rub the rope of the hammock against his body. If Sam arched his back a little, his cock would tease the light hairs of her pussy.

This battle of wills was no longer between Jess and Mrs Peters' training, but between her and Sam, to see who'd succumb to temptation and move first.

Chapter Eighteen

ROOM 54 STANK OF SEX. Its aroma filled every crevice. Into the silence, only punctuated by the shallow breath of the two players in Mrs Peters' game, the television screen flashed back on, and the echoes of past fucks swamped the room.

Jess assumed it was probably her getting screwed on the screen, but that didn't matter any more. What did matter was that she wasn't getting screwed at that very moment, and the sound of her past satisfaction was only making things worse.

She heard a whisper. She thought she'd imagined it at first, but there it was again. Jess opened her eyes and stared straight into Sam's. He was looking at her with an increased urgency, obviously trying to communicate without letting the unseen audience on the other side of the camcorder know.

Above the sound of the television Jess could barely hear him, but eventually she worked out he was saying, 'Let's move together.'

Struggling to keep her composure so she didn't give them away, Jess inclined her head a tiny fraction, hoping Sam would understand her acquiescence. She saw his left hand, cupped and hidden beneath his right, unfurl three fingers. He was going to count them down.

Three, two ... Jess readied herself to push all her

weight downwards, not sure if she'd actually be able to move the hammock within its pivot or not ... *one*.

Sam, rather than arch his back to reach her, shot his bound wrists upwards and clawed his fingers through the rope weave. As Jess wriggled and pushed down, he pulled hard, his muscles straining, until suddenly, a small creak indicated that their plan was working. With a final lurch, the pivot twisted and let out a piercing metallic squeal as the hammock moved with unaccustomed speed, crashing Jess on top of the artist with a blissfully heavy thump.

Crying out in anguished pain for her squashed and unbearably sore breasts, yet consumed with indescribable relief, Jess relished the sensation of male skin beneath her. Manoeuvring his arms clumsily between them, the artist positioned his fingers so they could flick and caress her nipples and breasts as best they could. Raising his hips, Sam bucked and squirmed until he had lined his cock up with Jess's cunt. With a sigh of, 'At last,' he pushed himself inside her, and with a simultaneous pinch of her right nipple, as Jess's fingers scrabbled away from the rope to rake over the sides of his body, they both came in a instant violent rush of long suppressed lust.

The single clap was long, drawn out and slow. 'Well done!' Mrs Peters voice was sarcastic, 'You both obviously have more initiative than I had credited you with. Clever – leaving me unsure who to blame. How can I possibly decide who broke first when you moved with such perfect simultaneous timing?'
Neither the artist nor the clerk spoke as, still on top of each other, the rope hammock stuck to them with sweat and come, they waited for Mrs Peters to finish her diatribe.

'I have no doubt, however, that when I play back the

tape and examine things more closely, I will see that Mr Wheeler was the initiator of this joint venture. You are not a stupid girl, Miss Sanders, but I believe you were too far down the line of desperation to have formed any sort of logical plan.'

As the manageress continued to stare down at her lover and administrator, she beckoned for Miss Sarah and Master Philips to approach and ease the players away from the hammock.

'You will shower, eat, and sleep. I will see you both in the Victorian Study at exactly 9 a.m. tomorrow.' Then Mrs Peters walked stiffly from the room, leaving Sam and Jess bruised, shaking with the aftermath of their climaxes and unprecedented tiredness, and each questioning their future with Mrs Peters and the Fables Hotel.

Dressed in her rather crumpled work suit, Jess winced as the cups of her cotton bra chaffed at the sides of her breasts, both of which had deep red welts surrounding them from the imprint of the rope hammock.

Despite two hot showers since the previous night, Jess's palms felt tacky with the perspiration of uncertainty. As she sat on the chaise longue in the study waiting for Mrs Peters to speak, she couldn't help but wonder if this was how criminals felt when the judge was about the deliver his verdict.

Mr Wheeler, more casually attired in clean clothes, sat next to Jess. She could feel the tension of what they'd shared the night before buzzing between them. Unlike her, though, his head was not bowed as he awaited their fate. He held his would-be lover's gaze with an unflinching confidence that Jess could only envy.

The manageress, freshly suited for a day's work, sat at the desk, her back straight, her head held high. Her expression was unreadable as she regarded her two projects with equal calm, as if she was a scientist deliberating the findings of a particularly complex experiment.

'Firstly, Miss Sanders.' Jess's stomach turned over and the familiar sensation of butterflies stormed through her system. 'You should know that, until you and Mr Wheeler colluded together and activated your orgasms, you lasted 43 minutes. That, I am pleased to say, is three and a half minutes longer than your predecessor.'

Jess felt a rush of pride as she listened, waiting to hear that she could now stay on the fifth floor, but instead Mrs Peters said, 'You may go to your desk. I am sure the work is piling up.'

Feeling totally wrong footed, Jess opened her mouth to ask if she'd be staying, but closed it again when she saw Mrs Peters was no longer paying her any attention. Standing, shaky from nerves, and still full of the uncertainty she'd nursed all night, Jess left the Victorian study behind her.

'That was a smart move in Room 54, Sam.' Laura Peters stood from behind her desk. 'Very clever.'

'Thank you.'

'I am beginning to see that in one respect I was quite wrong about you.'

'Is that so?' Sam stood too, and took a step towards the window seat where he'd been so unceremoniously restrained several hours before.

'You're no slave. We're equals. Your conniving with Miss Sanders proved that. I suggest we remain equals.'

The artist tilted his head. 'Which means what exactly?'

'You should come here and run the fifth floor with me. You have your guests, I'll have my guests, and we'll share guests, and train the staff together. Then, when the day's work is over, we can amuse each other.'

'I'm an artist and a graphic designer. I'm not a pro or a pimp.'

Laura Peters' gentle voice was suddenly edged with steel. 'And I am the manageress of a very successful hotel offering adult entertainment. I am not a prostitute or a pimp. NO ONE comes here or stays here unless they want to.'

'Point taken.' Sam looked from Laura to the view outside the velvet draped window. It didn't matter that his desk was overflowing with designs demanding his attention; he knew that would never satisfy him now. 'I will still paint, but otherwise I agree.'

The manageress nodded solemnly, before allowing the flicker of a smile to cross her face. 'Good.'

Confusion rattled around Jess's brain as she made her way to her small office. *Surely I can't have been sacked, or Mrs Peters wouldn't have sent me to the office to work? Am I staying here, but as a clerk? Could I cope with just being the office girl now that I've been through so much? I beat my predecessor's time, just as I was instructed to do. That should be enough – although I guess I cheated a bit. Did that make a difference? Will I be like Lee, a reserve for the fifth floor, but a hotel worker in the main?*

Jess's mind was still processing all the possibilities when she reached the office door. Miss Sarah was sitting on her seat.

'I need your help.'

'My help?' Jess's aching chest hardened as she regarded the woman before her.

'Yes. We are interviewing for your replacement this

afternoon, your knowledge of the job in question will be useful.'

'My replacement?' Jess's heart hammered faster. *So they are getting rid of me.*

'On this occasion Mrs Peters has agreed with the overall manager, Mr Davies, that an administrator with no connection to the top floor would be the best option, assuming you wouldn't mind taking responsibility for the fifth floor bookings. Part of your room will have to be used as an office between your hostess duties.

Jess's mouth opened and closed, but it was a few seconds before the words came out. 'I can stay?'

'Of course, Miss Sanders. We have been advertising your position for some time now.'

'But…?' Nonplussed, Jess tried to make sense of what she was hearing. 'Then why last night? Why all the tests if Mrs Peters had already decided to keep me on?'

Standing, Miss Sarah treated Jess to one of her rare smiles. 'Because it did you good, and you needed the experience. Plus, we wanted to make sure you weren't too good to be true. We all want to work with you, but if you'd known that, you might have relaxed and not worked nearly so hard to stay. Besides, you enjoyed it.'

'I …' Deciding against denying her enjoyment of the hammock experience, a strange mix of excited but terrified victory swept through Jess as she flicked a glance in her colleague's direction, before hastily dropping her eyes again. 'I thought you hated me, but then, after the time in your room, I wondered …' Jess found she couldn't finish the sentence, and was relieved when Miss Sarah cut in.

'Submissives like you are hard to find. You are attractive without being ridiculously thin, obedient, brave and willing to adapt. Your position on the fifth floor has been secure since you met Madam with me in the hospital room, but we had to be sure that you'd still want to stay once you'd been pushed to the limit.' Pulling at her short skirt to smooth it over her thighs, Miss Sarah moved towards the door, leaving a gob-smacked Jess staring after her. 'The interviews are at 2 p.m. I'd like you to attend.'

'Right.'

'Well, come on then.' The mistress smiled again, the gesture softening her angular features for a second as she held out her hand.

'Come on where?'

'To see your new room of course. Permanent employees of the fifth floor find it more convenient to live on site, and while we're there, I think it's high time you had another exercise class, it doesn't do to let these things slip.'

Doing her best not to grin like the proverbial Cheshire cat, Jess took the offered hand and lowered her eyes like the good little submissive she'd become. 'Of course, Miss Sarah.' Keeping the now familiar gush of longing between her legs a secret, for the moment at least …

Also from Xcite Books

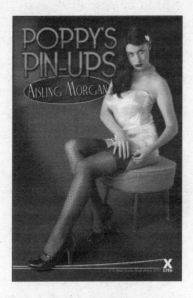

Poppy's Pin-ups
Aishling Morgan

The war is over, allowing Flying Officer Henry Truscott to concentrate on the far more important business of distributing much needed luxuries among the countries of the Mediterranean. Unfortunately people are getting back on their feet and prices are starting to drop, but with so many thousands of unattached young men about there is one commodity that can always be guaranteed a market, girls, or if not actual flesh and blood girls, then saucy pictures. Henry is more than happy to oblige on both counts, but when he signs up Corporal Poppy "Pinks" Pankhurst as his number two he finds he has bitten off rather more than he can chew, because her somewhat unorthodox ideas on discipline are only the start.

ISBN 9781908086068   £7.99

Saddled Up
Penny Birch

Amber Oakley is back! Determined as ever to avoid getting her bottom smacked but her own deep needs and the awkward circumstances she finds herself in trying to solve her financial difficulties mean otherwise.

Offering riding tuition to girls from wealthy families seems like a good idea, but Portia and Ophelia Crowthorne-Jones prove to have a few ideas of their own, and are soon indulging both their lesbian desires and their cruel sense of humour at Amber's expense. Will she end up as their plaything, or can she turn the tables and teach the little brats the lesson they so clearly deserve?

ISBN 9781907761843   £7.99

198

Students of Submission
Leigh Turner

Sally becomes one of eight university students hand-picked to participate in a financially rewarding social psychology experiment. At a secluded mansion, she meets the imperious "Director", Jane, who is to subject them to a series of challenges, more sexual than social. She realises she must hide some details of her recent history from Jane, but can she do this in the face of the increasingly perverted violations which rob her of will, as she succumbs more with each deliciously inventive pleasure, increasingly in thrall to the dominant older woman and her well versed staff?

ISBN 9781908766304   £7.99

Twelve Smarting Tails
Penny Birch

Penny Birch has been doing her best to keep readers of erotica happy since the release of *Penny in Harness* back in 1998. Since then she has treated her readership to 33 novels and more than 50 short stories, each and every one packed with truly filthy behaviour from a cast of characters unequalled in the world of erotic fiction. From spanking to pony-girl play, from plain old sex to some of the most bizarre scenarios ever created, Penny has provided it all, and in *Twelve Smarting Tails* offers up another dozen brand spanking new short stories. Each story is written from the viewpoint of one of her best known characters and focused on a favourite fetish, but there's one thing you can always guarantee, the girls get spanked!

ISBN 9781908766021   £7.99